# DEATH OF A DEALER

## D.P. Hart-Davis

MERLIN UNWIN BOOKS

First published in Great Britain by Merlin Unwin Books Ltd, 2024

Text © D.P. Hart-Davis 2024

Merlin Unwin Books Ltd
6 Rural Enterprise Centre
Eco Park Road
Ludlow
SY8 1FF

www.merlinunwin.co.uk

The author asserts their moral right to be identified with this work.
ISBN 978 1 913159 80 1
Typeset in Adobe Caslon Pro 12pt by Joanne Dovey,
Merlin Unwin Books
Printed by CPI Anthony Rowe England

*Also in the D.P. Hart-Davis country sports thriller series:*

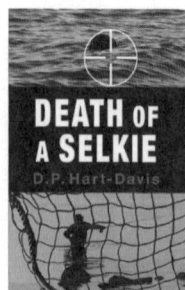

THE
STALKING
PARTY
D.P. Hart-Davis

DEATH OF A
HIGH FLYER
D.P. Hart-Davis

DEATH OF
A SELKIE
D.P. Hart-Davis

*Full details www.merlinunwin.co.uk*

*To my sisters-in-law,*
*Bridget, Lady Silsoe and Katie A Barstow*

# PRINCIPAL CHARACTERS

Jonah Murray, 36, amateur jockey and owner of Barleycourt Estate

Noel Murray, 34, his brother, horse dealer and bloodstock agent.

Helen Murray (née Robb), 26, who manages Barleycourt Livery Stables. Married to Noel, mother of Angus, 2

**Livery owners and clients**
Isabel Garraway, 32; Jasmine Dymoke, 35; Ricky Owen, 29; Anne Cutler, 32; Candy Cutler, 13; her daughter; Colonel Marshall, 53

**Stable staff**
John and Jeremy Conisby (twins) 42; Seamus Kenny, 40

**Hunt servants and officials**
Fergal Whyte, 50, huntsman; Harvey Joliffe, 25, amateur whipper-in; Marjorie Whittle, 46, hunt secretary and occasional Field Master; Jabez Crump, 56, terrierman

**Hunt saboteurs**
Fern Smith, 30; Piers Marshall, 20; Corky O'Sullivan, 31; Reuben Robins, 24

Jago Smith, 23, brother of Fern and groundsman at Confucius Centre

Mr Li, 48, Confucius Centre supervisor

William Yu, 36 Hong Kong dissident

Prudence Cutler, 35, Noel Murray's first wife

**Investigators**
DCI Robb, 47, Helen's father
Detective Sergeant Jim Winter, 30

# CHAPTER ONE

*'If you wake at midnight, and hear a horse's feet,*
*Don't go pulling back the blind and looking in the street.*
*Them as asks no questions Isn't told a lie...*

HELEN MURRAY JOLTED awake through mists of sleep, and wriggled on to her side to see the clock. Not midnight, but half past six on a dark November morning, and her alarm would not go off until seven, yet the drumming hoofs that had invaded her dream were still plainly audible, coming closer, threatening trouble.

Horses' legs are fragile. You must treat them like glass and never gallop on a road. How many times had her mother dinned that into her? There was something wrong in the galloping rhythm of these glass legs – a hesitancy, faltering, a missed beat, a missing shoe? Hard to place but it didn't sound good. She remembered old Silas, her childhood's ruddy-faced farrier, chanting in time with his ringing strokes on the anvil: *'T'aint 'untin' on t' 'ill as 'urts an 'oss's 'oofs, but 'ammer, 'ammer, 'ammer on t' 'ard 'igh road.'* But this was no hammering trot, it was a panicky gallop along the potholed tarmac of the back drive, coming rapidly closer.

Could it be one of theirs? She was sure she had checked that all the doors were securely bolted on her late-night round.

5

Some horses like fiddling with the catches, but she'd never known one let himself out. Besides, there were kick-over safety latches at the bottom of each door, which no horse could reach by leaning over.

Hurry, hurry. Jeans, sweatshirt, muck-boots, fleece and she was out of the lodge door, running down the path that led to the stables.

In the big house, a light flicked on and seconds later her mobile chirruped. Jonah, her boss and brother-in-law, a whip-thin and fearless amateur jockey who could ride at 11 stone but whose movements were currently restricted after a crashing fall at Towcester. 'Hels? What's up? Sounds like a loose horse…'

'Don't worry. I'm on my way. Call you in a mo.'

She slowed to a walk as she neared the handsome high arch of the coach house, and beyond it the stable yard with its three sides of loose boxes and fourth made up of tack room, feed shed, smithy, wash area and barn. The grand arched entrance under the clock tower dominated one end, and to the left a back way led in via a cattle grid and locked gate. Two horse lorries and a trailer were parked under a roof and the high, squared-off muck heap – handyman Seamus' pride – steamed gently in its concrete enclosure.

Fifteen boxes were occupied: five with her own horses, plus seven paying liveries, and three do-it-yourselfers; all upset, restive, pawing their beds and box-walking, then returning to hang over their half-doors and strain towards the cattle grid and gate leading to the back drive.

'All right now, boys and girls. Take it easy,' she said, forcing herself to sound calm though the drumming hoofs were very close. She couldn't see the approaching runaway because a trailer blocked her view, but clearly he was making straight for the grid. Oh, God! If he tries to jump that…

She sprinted for the gate beside the grid, unlocked it and flung it open, and at the last possible moment the horse jinked through, striking sparks from the cobbled surround. For an instant she thought he was down, but he found an extra leg, righted himself, and clattered to a shuddering halt in the middle of the yard. Blasting a snort through red-rimmed nostrils, he gave a ringing neigh, then wheeled as if to continue his frantic progress through the archway and into the park beyond.

Suleiman: I might have known, she thought. Suleiman the Magnificent, the Anglo-Arab dressage star who belonged in the double-sized stallion-box at the end of the line where he could see all the activity of the yard. Seven years old and worth his weight in gold, but now wild-eyed and beyond reason, his chestnut coat foaming and dark with sweat.

'Whoa, there. Steady, steady. There's a fella. Easy, now. Easy,' she soothed, stepping up to him and quietly taking hold of a trailing rein. 'Good boy, you're all right. Come on, now.'

She stroked his neck and tried to lead him across to his box, but he jibbed, head high, bracing his weight backwards. A dark stain had begun to pool under his near fore.

A rattle over the cattle grid announced the arrival of reinforcements: Jeremy and John Conisby, short, bandy-legged bachelor twins who lived in the gate lodge matching her own at the far end of the drive. They propped their bikes against the wall and approached cautiously.

'Switch on the main light, Jem,' she called.

A moment later blue fluorescence flooded the yard and she saw what she dreaded: a six-inch flap of skin torn from Suleiman's chest and extending under his belly, with who knew how deep a wound behind it.

Blood was pouring steadily down his foreleg, and now the stimulus of flight was gone pain was replacing it, making him shift from leg to leg, unwilling to put weight on any of them.

'Best get him inside, missus, and see what's what,' murmured John, stroking and shushing as he took the other rein.

Leading, pushing, coaxing, the three persuaded Suleiman to hop over to his stable, where the extent of the damage became clear.

As well as the torn brisket, his shiny golden skin was crisscrossed with scratches and minor lacerations as if he had galloped through brambles, one hind shoe was missing, and a lump on his forehead hinted at a collision with a branch. He relaxed as they checked him over, head now hanging low and belly drawn up…

'Miss Garraway's going to go mad when she sees him,' said John. 'Good job she's away.'

'You can say that again,' Helen muttered, speed-dialling the vet. Engaged. Hell! Was it an emergency? Yes. A pause, click-click, and a message to say she was being transferred.

Of all her livery owners, Isabel Garraway was the most demanding and difficult. The only daughter of a shipping magnate's third marriage, thirty-two-year-old Isabel was rich, fussy, and unpredictable. She was used to getting her own way – a thin, wishy-washy, strawberry blonde with a sharp nose, an iron will and a high little-girl voice that rose to a shrill scream at any hint of opposition. She was in love – or imagined she was – with Jonah Murray, and Helen wondered if she didn't know or just wouldn't accept the fact that Jonah was wedded to the single life and had no intention of being tied to anyone.

Not my business, anyway, she decided. That's something she'll have to work out for herself.

Nothing was too good for Isabel's horse, and nothing too much trouble for the stable staff. Suleiman had special forage, special bedding, a special diet including additives and supplements for every condition from which any horse had ever suffered; boosters, calmers, powders, ointments; a wardrobe to rival a beauty queen's, and the finest saddlery money could buy. Suleiman never left the yard without overreach boots and knee-pads, and when he travelled to competitions in his own luxurious horse-trailer, it took the best part of an hour to dress him in padded hood, padded rugs, bandages and tail-guard. Like an American racehorse, he had his own nannie, Sarah, a small phlegmatic donkey, who accompanied him to shows and without whom he could be difficult.

Suleiman was, in the stable staff's view, a bleeding nuisance, but at the same time as griping about Isabel's demands they were secretly proud to have him.

'T'aint 'is fault she fusses so,' John summed up the general feeling, and they were at least a little chuffed by being entrusted with such a magnificent addition to the yard. Everyone knew that Suleiman had been summarily removed from the care of at least three other stables which had not come up to Isabel's standards.

'Sent a box to pick 'im up without so much as a by-your-leave,' said Jeremy darkly. 'Me mate as works for Lady Blackler told me they never 'eard a dickeybird till arter 'e'd gone.'

That was why it was only under extreme pressure that Helen had agreed to board him at livery for the winter. The pressure had been partly financial – you pays for what you gets and the business could always do with money – and partly from her boss.

Jonah found Isabel's fixation on him harmless, even amusing. 'Oh, I think we should let her keep him here for a bit. Call it payback for her keeping the Hunt afloat.'

'How long is a bit?' she said carefully.

He glanced at her stony face and said, 'I know Izzy's not everyone's cup of tea but I've always felt sorry for her. She had an awful childhood, poor girl: constantly on the move, changing schools, chivvied from place to place. Stepmothers, half-brothers, half-sisters – difficult to know who was family and who wasn't – and there's no denying the old Brig was a bully. He could be an absolute tyrant.'

'I thought he was a friend of yours.'

Jonah had laughed and wrinkled his nose. 'Hardly!'

'But…'

'Oh, I know I used to ride his horses. He put me up on some good ones, too. But that's not the same as being a friend. Like with all bullies, you had to stand up to him: tell him where he got off. Poor little Izzy couldn't do that.' He paused and thought for a moment. 'Tell you what, Hels. We'll keep this precious horse of hers for six months, let her have a bit of fun with him over the winter. She can use the school – bring her own personal trainer…' He laughed, 'Honestly, Hels! Your face! Then next summer she can take him to these competitions she's always talking about…'

'But she can't ride one side of him!' wailed Helen before she could stop herself.

'Miaow!'

'It's true. When Noel rides him he's a different horse.'

'Your husband puts a couple of thousand on a horse's value just by throwing a leg over him,' said Jonah with no trace of fraternal envy. It was true. Even the most placid old plodder would arch his neck and grow a couple of inches the moment Noel was in the saddle. Jonah added, 'Why else should I keep him here eating his head off and let him do all the buying and selling?'

'Just tell me, Jonah, what *did* Isabel pay for Suleiman?'

'That's a dark secret.'

'But I want to know.'

'And I honestly can't tell you. She had to buy two people out

– I know that – and she did own one leg of him already, but as to what she actually paid, your guess is as good as mine. Think of a number and treble it and you may be in the right area.'

'Just for a horse…?'

'A very special horse. And he's a stallion, which puts his value into the stratosphere. So if Izzy wants to keep him here and ride him in competitions, well – that's OK by me.' He held up a hand. 'No, don't argue. I've decided.'

'Half your staff will walk out.'

'I'd be surprised if they did. Money talks, you know, and if Isabel stopped paying its bills the Hunt would have to shut up shop. When does Noel get back, by the way?'

For once she knew. 'He's got a busy week. Goff's sales on Wednesday, Dubai on Thursday; then he's due to go to a big dinner in London – Bloodstock Owners' beano of some kind – on Friday night; back here to hunt next Saturday.'

Jonah had laughed. 'Par for the course, eh?'

She thought back to that conversation while she and John were gently cleaning and disinfecting Suleiman's many lacerations. His thousand-pound saddle had suffered too, wrenched over to one side with the same deep scratches across the expensive black hide and a long bramble sucker caught under the flap. One stirrup and its leather was missing, pulled from its bar, no doubt, when the rider fell. Who had that rider been? Who would have had the sheer audacity to nick one of their horses in the dim pre-dawn gloom and ride him away – where? Into the woods? To a lorry waiting in a lay-by with its lights doused and ramp down?

Fury rose like a choking black constriction in her throat – fear and fury. It was so easy to take a horse, who had been trained since birth to follow where humans led, to do what humans asked him to. She forced it down: this was no time to give way to emotion.

Horrible even to think it, but one of their staff must be involved. The tack room was locked at night but it was an open secret that the key was kept on a nail behind a bin in the feed shed; and each horse's tack was neatly hung from a labelled saddle-rack for easy identification.

'Best make the vet get a move on,' said John, still sponging the chest wound. 'This flap of skin – it needs stitching.'

'It's Saturday. I got the emergency service and they always take longer. We'll make him comfortable and then I'll start ringing round.'

Vet. Doctor. Possibly police as well.

'Unting morning, too.'

'Don't rub it in.'

Hunting mornings had to be planned with military precision. Timetables. Spreadsheets. Careful briefing of personnel. Everyone involved knew what had to be done and when, but there was always the chance of a slip which could throw the whole schedule.

'Ow many going out today?'

She reckoned on her fingers and said, 'A lorryload. Democrat's not right yet, so Ricky Owen's taking my black mare. Should be no problems there. Jasmine wants a short day on Betsinda…'

'First time out, eh?' said John with the slight sideways twitch of his mouth that passed for a smile.

'I know. I warned her she might have a rough ride, but she said it was now or never. Then Colonel Marshall asked if he could hire Master Mariner.'

She paused and John gave her a searching look. 'Was that 'is son got bound over last week? Saw it in *The Gazette*. Looked a right 'alf-portion of misery. Long hair, long beard, called summat daft: Woody, was it?'

'Fungus.'

'Ah, that's right. Fungus it was. So 'e's the Colonel's son. You'd never guess.'

Helen sighed. 'That's him all right. Silly bugger: high time he grew up. Bit of a thorn in the flesh for the family.'

Fungus and a cohort of scruffy boys and girls had made a Town Hall demonstration against climate change which ended with three police cars being dented and fines all round. She wondered if the Colonel had bailed his son out or if he washed his hands of him. It wasn't the kind of thing you could ask.

She said to John, 'So that's two of my horses going out, plus Jasmine with Betsinda, and maybe one of the DIYs will want to hitch a ride. You'll drive them – OK? I topped up the tank yesterday. The Meet's at eleven, over at Mounteford Common, so it won't take more than half an hour, forty minutes max, to get there. I'll have to stay here until we get the vet's verdict. Then we'll try to work out exactly what happened. If I can, I'll bring the trailer and join you.'

This was a faint hope, she knew. Mounteford Common was one of her favourite meets, a wide, rolling expanse of heath and scrubland rising out of the Chiltern beechwoods, but by the time she had dealt with all the problems arising from Suleiman's escapade, the huntsman would more likely be blowing for Home than drawing the last covert.

Now the car park was filling: the usual morning bustle. Feeding, watering, skipping out. Carrot-topped Seamus with the big muck-trailer hitched behind his diminutive tractor, collecting the contents of the skips. Everyone temporarily too busy to ask questions, but word was going round, she knew, from the worried faces and looks cast towards Suleiman's loose box. Security. No one wanted to keep a horse where it might vanish overnight like poor Shergar, the Derby winner who had been kidnapped by the IRA and never seen again. What else could they do to keep the horses safe? More sophisticated locks. CCTV. Guard dogs brought their own problems and the expense of human guards put them out of the question. She didn't want to turn the whole place into a fortress.

I'll have to have another go at Jonah, she thought. When he hears about this he'll have to listen to me and see it's just not on to have such a valuable animal in the yard. Isabel had won the three-sided bidding war when Suleiman was put up for sale: now it was up to her to take care of him.

As if by psychic communication, her mobile rang again. She dropped the pad of gamgee she was holding into a bucket and fumbled for her phone. Jonah.

'What's the problem? Have you got it sorted?'

'The problem,' she said crisply, 'is that someone tried to steal Suleiman. That was him galloping on the drive.'

There was a shocked silence, then he said, 'Someone who didn't know about Sarah, I imagine. How is he? Any damage?'

She relayed a list of the cuts and scratches and added, 'I've called the vet – McAndrew's on duty but he's out on a job. I'm just waiting for him to ring back.'

'No damage to his wedding tackle?'

'Not as far as I can see.'

'That's one plus, at least. Oh, by the way, your lad's awake. I can hear him over the intercom, grizzling for his mum. Shall I get him up? Keep him amused until breakfast?'

'Would you?' she said guiltily, 'I'm afraid it means...'

'Come on, Hels. I'm perfectly capable of changing a nappy, and time's ticking on. I'll deal with young Gus, and you finish the horses. Then you can bring me up to date.'

He rang off and she said to John, 'That's about all we can do for now. Give him a small feed and leave him in peace. I never thought I'd say this, but thank God for Sarah. If the thief – thieves – had got Suleiman into a lorry or trailer, they could be miles away by now. He could be hidden on a farm, in a barn, in a garage – anywhere, and we wouldn't have a clue where to begin looking for him.' She drew a deep breath and squared her shoulders. 'Now I'd better go and tell everyone what's happened before the rumour mill gets to work.'

Barleycourt Manor, a thousand-acre estate encircled by the ever-changing, ever-beautiful beechwoods to the north of Marlow, had been in a ruinous condition when Jonah and Noel's far-sighted grandfather snapped it up at the end of World War II.

Time, weather, and a double whack of death duties had taken their toll on the big house, but the grand stable yard had survived as it was built, and though judicious selling of land had reduced the estate to a more manageable six hundred acres, principally pasture, it was now ideally suited to the current owners' preoccupation with buying, selling, and training horses, besides riding them in races and competitions for the fun of it, while Helen's growing livery business made a small but steady contribution to the Barleycourt finances.

*****

With rain clouds lowering and the wind getting up, it was no surprise that by two forty-five some of their less fit liveries were trickling back into the yard. People who rode only once or twice a week hadn't the stamina to stay with hounds more than three hours, as Fergal the long-serving huntsman well knew. So long as they got an early gallop and half a dozen jumps they were perfectly content to return to their lorries after hounds had drawn a few coverts, particularly if they realised the pack was heading away from home. Falls, refusals, or slight injuries to horse or rider would have accounted for more early quitters, and a high proportion of weekend sportsmen would simply have become lost in unfamiliar lanes and fields and be glad of a lift home.

'I'll 'ave the box 'ere until one-thirty,' John would have told them on arrival at the Meet. 'Anyone as 'ad enough by then is welcome to come 'ome along o' me, and me brother will come out to fetch the rest later. That suit everyone?'

It did. Fainthearts or those unsure how their horses would behave in company were reassured that they would not be abandoned: it was only a question of finding their way back to the Meet.

Wily Colonel Marshall, who had coughed up £90 for the pleasure of riding Master Mariner, Helen's bold, raking grey pointer, took a look at the sky and decided to hoard his energy for the afternoon when hounds were likely to draw Southcott Furze, where he and the Hunt handyman had spent a whole weekend building a lovely line of fences. What fun it would be to jump them! He would potter along at the back shutting gates and talking to the terriermen until most of the Field went home, and then heyho for the Furze.

Do-It-Yourself livery owner and anaesthetist Jasmine Dymoke, elegant in her well-cut dark-blue coat with twinkling Hunt buttons, was not planning to let her young mare do much galloping. 'I've just brought Betsinda along to see hounds,' she explained to the Colonel in gasps between bucks, as they trotted away from the Meet. 'She finds it all too, too thrilling.'

Naughty Betsinda would also have preferred to join the vanguard rather than being kept well clear of hounds, and made her wishes known by humping her back, snatching at her bit and progressing sideways.

Should have given her five miles on the road instead of bringing her over in the lorry, thought the Colonel, as Betsinda cannoned into his horse for the third time. Seeing hounds! She'll see the thong of my whip if she kicks good old Mariner. He edged away from the over-excited mare in order to talk to the Hunt Secretary, neat, bespectacled Marjorie Whittle, about an extra ticket for the Hunt Ball. She was *distraite*, eyes scanning the Field for stray Caps she might have missed at the Meet.

He said, 'Did you hear about the shemozzle at Barleycourt this morning? Someone tried to steal that showy stallion of Isabel's. Tacked him up and rode away before it was light.'

'Never!' Now he had her full attention.

'Don't know all the details yet. Helen was pretty tight-lipped, but no doubt we'll hear all about it later.'

Many and various are the reasons that people ride to hounds, but a desire to kill foxes barely figures in them. Some go to see and be seen, to show off their horses and possibly sell them; some crash-and-dash merchants are there for the thrill of galloping and jumping, and others for the rare pleasure of riding over fields and woods from which they would otherwise be excluded. Some are content to jog around lanes and through gates, while others think nothing of tackling a stone wall straight off the road if it will win them half a field's advantage. Some spend the whole day in a state of ecstasy, and others of suppressed terror. Point-to-point jockeys, who need a Master's signature to confirm that their racehorse has been fairly hunted, slouch along at the back of the Field, praying for 2 o'clock when the desired scribble will free them to go home.

As a result, a Field of sixty might be whittled down to a hard core of a dozen or so when the sky darkens, the temperature drops, and the best of the day's hunting can begin. Until then Colonel Marshall thought he would simply enjoy Mariner's good manners and springy paces, the beauty of the winter landscape, the glorious pageant of hounds and horses streaming across the valley bottom and jumping its little brook, together with the comedy of those who failed to jump it. He might catch a loose horse. He might rescue a pretty girl who had lost hounds and reunite her with them. But all the time he would be saving Mariner's energy and his own for the last hour of the afternoon when they headed for Southcott Furze.

Of course they might not go there. That was one of the glories of hunting: you could never predict what would happen because the fox – in the person of the trail-layer – was in charge. Fergal the huntsman might plan where he wanted to go, and end up miles off course, his horse blown and his whipper-in collecting hounds in the half dark in unfamiliar territory. That didn't often happen – Fergal knew his country inside out – but it *could* happen, and the thrill of trying to stay with hounds over strange obstacles in unknown country was something that sustained you throughout the bleakest winter.

And if he found himself benighted far from his transport, he had the comforting assurance that the iPhone in his pocket, so despised when his daughter first gave it to him, was one modern invention that amply earned its place in every hunting man's kit.

The long, melancholy, undulating note of *Gone to Ground* hung for a moment in the damp air as Colonel Marshall patted Mariner's shoulder and winked at Marjorie Whittle, the only other remaining member of the Field. Clouds of steam rose from the horses after the headlong, exhilarating gallop over the new fences, which had more than repaid the trouble taken to build them.

'Just what we needed after all that faffing about in Oxlease Larches,' he muttered. 'Think I'll call it a day or I'll get it in the neck from the wife.'

Fergal was standing in his stirrups, checking the pack. 'All on,' he said with satisfaction, and a moment later fat little Harvey Joliffe, computer geek and amateur whipper-in, echoed, 'All on.'

The Colonel offered his flask round and took a pull himself, then gathered up his reins. 'Good night,' he said formally, though it was barely half past four.

'Good night,' Marjorie responded with a smile. Good old Willie, she thought, looking after him as he rode away: neat, square-shouldered, every inch a cavalryman. He does love his hunting. Shame that son of his doesn't take after him. All talk and no trousers, as they say. Brilliant shot, though. Should have forced him into the army instead of letting him fiddle around with leftie politics. Or he could have been a jockey, if he'd had the nerve. Right build for it.

She sighed. Her own son had longed to ride in races, but his weight was against him. Twelve stone at fourteen, and goodness knows what her poor daughter-in-law now had to spend in shoe leather.

The Colonel lit a cigarette and considered his options. The fun at the Furze had been well worth the extra miles it had added to the hack home. Mariner was fit as a flea and could do it all again, and Dora – bless her – had agreed to drive their own trailer to the Red Lion at Wystan Green and box up in the car park there, so the horse would be back in his stable by six.

An idea occurred to him. Instead of slogging three miles along the verge, with cars whizzing past, it would surely make more sense to cut back across the far corner of the Furze again to where it shared a boundary with the playing fields of that poncy new international school which had bought Dene Park off the old Misses Rigby recently. He had a vague memory of Marjorie Whittle getting a letter informing her that the Hunt would no longer be welcome in the school grounds, but quietly hacking home wasn't the same as hunting, was it? And who was likely to be playing hockey at dusk on a November evening?

He continued along the verge for a few hundred yards, then checked his bearings. Somewhere along here there was a bridle gate on to the track that skirted the school buildings – ah, here it was – and now he had only to hop over a narrow stile – obligingly Mariner hopped – and he was riding across the shamefully neglected outfield of what had once been cricket pitches.

He kept a sharp eye out for trouble, but no one challenged him. Indeed, he was pretty sure no one had seen him leave the road. Lights were on in a long wooden building that could have been a gym or lecture hall, and once a door opened, letting a flood of light stream across the grass, but keeping Mariner well into the shadow of the overgrown hedge, he continued on his way, heading for the gate into Southcott Furze.

It was locked: damn! Locked with a chain and a thumping great padlock. What's more, some accursed gardener or groundsman had reversed the top hinge so that it could not be lifted off. Damn and double damn!

Now his idea of a shortcut seemed less appealing, but he still didn't want to retrace his footsteps. Never jump on the way home is hunting's sensible maxim, but when circumstances demand there are exceptions to every rule, and Mariner was a copybook jumper.

Make up your mind, he urged himself.

The gate was old-fashioned: wooden, heavy, five-barred. Not the uninviting metal seven-barred type with adjustable hinges that he had often shied away from, but the kind of obstacle most horses would make nothing of. The light was going. He couldn't hang about here much longer.

He showed Mariner the middle of the gate to indicate what was expected of him, wheeled to take a short run, sat well down and set him at it. Mariner tucked his forelegs up neatly and rose with a leap that would have cleared the gate by a foot when a sudden dazzle of white light caught him full in the eyes. Blinded, he dropped his hind legs on the top bar with a splintering crash, and the Colonel felt himself falling...falling...

That's torn it, was his last thought as the ground rose up to meet him.

*****

'Is everyone back now?' asked Helen at six o'clock, pushing open the tackroom door and releasing a heady aroma of woodsmoke, saddle soap and sweat into the frosty night air. Hunting debrief was usually an agreeable ritual, with everyone glowing from the day's exertions, horses bedded down for the night, snifters scavenged from flasks and Mars bars from sandwich cases to share around. Tonight she was greeted by a chorus of disapproval...

'Shut that door, for crying out loud!' called Ricky Owen, whose Intermediate eventer was temporarily out of action, reducing him to hiring Helen's black mare. 'We've only just got up a decent fug in here. Now, are you going to put us out of our agony and tell all or must we go on guessing?'

'I would if I could, believe me.' She rubbed her eyes. It had been a long day. The vet had come, stitched, shot Suleiman full of LA antibiotics, and promised to return tomorrow. The police had been and gone. Isabel Garraway's mobile wasn't answering, and little Gus was cutting a molar.

She counted heads. John and Jeremy in identical dark-blue sweatshirts and Puffa jackets sat next to the tackroom stove, fiddling with the draught, their eyes anxious. They were always first to arrive, last to leave the stable yard, and they felt today's security near-miss as a personal affront.

'Any trouble at the Meet?' she asked.

Lanky Ricky Owen, estate agent and keen eventer, who could tuck his long legs to a jockey's crouch when racing, but schooled young horses with leathers so long he might have tied them under his mount's belly, now sat with them doubled under him on a saddle-horse, rhythmically burnishing a curb-chain. 'Sabs?' he said with a grin. 'I think they were… er… misdirected.'

'By you?'

'Well…er…There was a bunch of them in The Feathers last night. I may have dropped a hint which they took the wrong way.'

Jasmine Dymoke gave a squeal of laughter. She had dealt with her saddlery, boots, and muddy coat by dumping it all on the washroom floor and turning the hose on it. Tomorrow would be time enough for further cleaning operations. Now she appointed herself hostess, offering round what remained in her basket of iron rations.

'Go on, Hels,' she urged. 'Have a handful of Haribos. Top up your blood sugar, pet. You've had a horrid shock and anyway I can't take this lot home or the lovely Elsa will think I don't appreciate her efforts.' The lovely Elsa was her enormous Afro-Caribbean housekeeper of whom everyone at Barleycourt was deeply jealous. 'Come on, boys, eat up. You're not doing your bit.'

'Don't mind if we do,' said the twins, grinning and taking, but Ricky waved the offer away.

'Tell us about this morning,' he said seriously. 'What did the police say?'

Helen grimaced. 'Not much.'

The police had been slow, ponderous, clearly uninterested. They looked over the half-door at Suleiman, now rugged and bandaged, and briefly examined the yard's various lights and locks. Nothing wrong that they could see. A horse had gone missing but had returned of his own accord. OK, so what's the problem? No amount of emphasis on Suleiman's value could change this attitude, nor did the question of the missing stirrup intrigue them.

'Bound to turn up,' the bored constable had said, clicking shut his iPhone. 'Place like this – it could be anywhere.' He gave Helen an incident number and drove off, eager to get away from this curious world where a horse which looked to him like any other could cost as much as a whole row of houses.

'Before I begin, are we all here? I don't want to go through it twice.'

'Everyone's back except Colonel Marshall,' reported Jasmine. 'He asked me to tell you he'd make his own way home from Southcott.'

'Quite a way to hack,' said Ricky, glancing at the darkened window and Jasmine gave her tinkling laugh.

'I think he planned to whistle up Dora with a trailer and wait for her in the nearest pub.'

'Up to him,' said Helen briskly. 'OK, we won't wait. I'll tell you what I know but I warn you it's not much. Anything you can add may help. *Oh!*'

She spun round, for the door behind her banged open, and before Ricky had even opened his mouth to protest, Jonah came hopping through, supported by his crutch. Close on his heels followed thirteen-year-old Candy Cutler, who kept two showjumping ponies as DIY liveries, and often babysat Gus for extra funds. Her long black ponytail swung and her almond eyes shone as she skipped along, and her round cheeks were pink with excitement as well as cold.

'Jonah!' It was the first time he had managed the transit from house to stable yard.

'Look what Candy picked up in the park,' he said, sweeping aside the tack-cleaning clutter to clear a space on the table for what he was carrying. Everyone stared at it in silence.

The missing leather had its stirrup-iron still attached normally, but a brown jodhpur boot had twisted so that it jammed against the bars, clear evidence that someone had fallen off and been dragged. Someone who could still be lying injured in the park. Injured or...dead?

A woman's boot, thought Helen, feeling suddenly sick. A pale blue cashmere sock inside. Could it be...? Was it possible that Isabel had decided to remove her own horse without a word of warning? After all, she had done so before. Was the story of a wedding in France just a blind?

'Jago found it, not me,' said Candy, blushing furiously. Her mother did not approve of twenty-three-year-old Jago. Too old, too handsome, and far too interested in her little girl. He worked as groundsman for the Confucius Centre, but liked to hang around stables, doing odd jobs and picking up gossip. As a former helper at the local Farm Animal Veterinary practice, he considered himself an expert on animal health, but among the Barleycourt livery owners, only Candy ever took his advice. 'He was bringing in the ponies for me and saw it glinting in the grass.'

She looked round at all the solemn faces. 'D'you know whose it is?'

Jonah nodded slowly. 'We'd better organise a search party,' he said.

# CHAPTER TWO

AS SOON AS he pushed open the door of Fern Smith's studio, Piers Marshall knew that he'd come at the wrong time. Sitting cross-legged on the bare boards, hands on knees, back straight and eyes unfocused, she was listening to a disembodied voice urging her to empty her mind, let her spirit roam free, shake off the material world, and he was well aware that however interesting his news, she would pay it no attention until the tape released her.

Even then it might be another hour before she was fully functional again. Yoga sessions seemed to leave her in a vaguely benevolent dream, disconnected from such mundane matters as talking to flatmates or cooking supper.

'Fern...' he said tentatively.

No response beyond an upward flash of the eyes.

He mooched through into the tiny kitchen, dismayed but not surprised to see the morning's bowls and mugs heaped in the sink, and the shelf that served as a table still smeared with coffee-mug rings, jam and breadcrumbs. A heap of ripped envelopes had their contents shoved back inside them: he recognised a headed letter from the District Council, and one written in green ink which was probably a complaint about noise or dog mess from one of their neighbours.

It was at times like this that he seriously questioned the wisdom of leaving the comforts of home to live here, but Fern and his stepmother did not see eye to eye, and he had made his choice. To delay the moment of starting the dishwashing, he picked up a copy of *Sabbing News* and his attention was immediately caught by a picture of himself on the cover, mouth open in what had probably been a defiant shout but which made him look like a gaffed fish, with a undersized female PCSO holding his arm behind his back. Not quite the heroic image he had hoped for, but at least it must have shown Fern and her mates that far from being a poor little rich boy as they taunted, he was a serious Sab and prepared to suffer for the cause. *Huntsman's Son Fined* said the caption, which was nonsense because there was a big difference between being a *huntsman* and *riding to hounds*, which he knew well – though presumably subs on *Sabbing News* did not. He wondered if Pa had seen the report.

He flicked through the paper, finding nothing else of interest, and had just started running water into the sink when the ingratiating voice next door was abruptly cut off, and Fern stumbled through into the kitchen, still slightly dazed and glassy eyed.

'Time for drinkies,' she suggested. 'Is the water hot? You can leave all that and do it later.'

The water was barely tepid: thankfully he abandoned the sink and joined her at the table, pushing the photograph towards her like a dog offering its ball. 'Recognise him?'

She glanced at it and laughed. 'You look a right prat, shouting and bawling for attention. Wrong tactics, dude. Doesn't do to get yourself noticed too much.'

'But I thought you said…'

'Wrong again. Keep under the radar's my advice. I'm too well known around these parts. The fuzz always picks on me

— *Death of a Dealer* —

for choice,' she said with a certain complacency, pulling back her long red hair and admiring her profile in the mirror beside the stove.

'I was only trying to do my bit,' he said humbly.

'You stick to what I say and you'll be all right. You're what they call a cleanskin, new to the game, so keep it that way as long as you can.'

Cleanskin. It sounded like a cure for acne.

She was thirty, ten years older than him, and veteran of many a demo, for whom a night in the cells held no terrors. She would join any march, riot, or protest that involved banners, smashed windows, cocking a snook at authority. Hunting was her particular bugbear.

'Smug bastards. All dolled up in their red coats to chase poor little foxes. Make 'em sweat,' she'd say, as she sprayed Anti Mate in the eyes of a passing foxhound and Piers tried not to wince. It was no good going soft: other sabs could be far more brutal. Their tactics varied: some threw down nails and screws in muddy gateways, hoping to lame horses. Some let down the tyres of parked horse lorries, or sprayed glue in locks. Their star turn was Corky, who could blow a horn, and bring hounds pouring out of any covert they were drawing, much to the irritation to their huntsman. One had been prosecuted for stretching a tripwire across a woodland ride, though in Fern's view that was a step too far.

'That's dangerous. Criminal... Puts people off. Got to get the public on our side, that's the way we'll have hunting banned for good.'

'You telling me how to get it banned?' Behind her the door had opened and Corky O'Sullivan himself swaggered through, earrings and nose-ring glinting, long crinkly hair caught back in a ponytail. His tattered cargo shorts hung down below his knees, within inches of muddy army boots.

He wrenched open the fridge door and helped himself to a blackened banana.

'How did it go?' said Fern eagerly.

'It didn't. Bloody waste of time.'

She frowned. 'What d'you mean? What happened?'

'Couldn't find it for a start. That's to say, we found the Common, all right, but not a sign of horses, dogs, anything like a hunt.'

'But where were the people? The lorries? You can't hide those.'

'Bastards had parked in a field behind the church, and a bunch of heavies had taped off the verge for half a mile beyond it. Told us we couldn't stop there. We'd be obstructing the road, and anyway it was private land.'

'But it's a *Common*,' said Fern hotly... 'Commons belong to everyone.'

'Not this one, it seems. By the time we finished arguing with the rozzers, the hunt had gone. Given us the slip.' He threw the banana skin in the general direction of the bin. 'Never saw them again.'

'But all the stuff I gave you about where they were going after the Common?'

'Total b.s. Either the bloke in The Feathers didn't know his arse from his elbow, or he was having you on.'

Fern shook her head. 'He told me he'd be there himself. He *must* have known.'

'Then you'd better stop believing everything you're told in pubs, sweetie.' Corky shrugged, indifferent. The banana had partially restored his blood sugar and he enjoyed her indignation. She was such a know-all. She thought she'd got the whole thing taped, cosying up to men in bars and pumping them for info. Well, last night someone had clearly spotted her as an anti and gone out of his way to mislead her.

Remembering the day's humiliating failure to find, let alone disrupt the hunt, he gritted his teeth and began banging open cupboard doors in search of something else to eat.

She talked as though keeping up with people on horses was a walk in the park. OK, let her try chasing them along muddy farm tracks and over half-frozen plough, and she'd soon change her tune. It was all very well saying she'd had enough of the limelight and would collect intelligence covertly, but judging by today's fiasco the only thing she had collected was a load of rubbish, and they could do without that.

'Hey! That's my supper you're eating,' said Fern as he dug into a pot of yoghourt, and Piers made a mental note to try the chippy on the corner before he closed at eight.

'Won't be a mo,' he said, making for the door, but Corky wasn't done yet.

'Hang on. You haven't heard the best of it. We may not have had a go at the hunt, but Fern's little bro found an old bloke trespassing in the grounds of that Chinese school, and got a good shot. I've downloaded it – wait one… Should be worth a bit in terms of publicity.'

Fern regarded him sceptically. 'How d'you know he was a hunter?'

'Wearing the same rig, wasn't he? Gate was locked so he tried to jump it. Look here.'

He scrolled rapidly through dozens of images, muttering, then zoomed and showed it to Fern.

'Jago says he smashed the gate and came a right cropper.'

'Was he hurt?' she asked.

'Dunno. Jago said a whole load of people came to see what the noise was, and the horse ran off into the trees, but the gate was matchwood. Take a bit of explaining, that will,' he said with satisfaction.

'Let's see.' Pushing forward, Piers looked over her shoulder and his mouth dried. Against a dark background, Master Mariner's dappled face and folded forelegs loomed directly towards the camera, and between those cocked ears, leaning forward and perfectly recognisable, was Colonel Marshall.

He gasped and Fern eyed him narrowly. 'What's up, Fungus?'

Piers licked his lips and swallowed, finding it difficult to speak. He pointed to the photograph.

'That – that's my dad.'

*****

Promptly at nine next morning, as Helen opened her laptop in the office she shared with Jonah, her mobile chirruped.

'Izzy here,' said the high, little-girl voice, and Helen's heart gave a great bump of relief, followed by a wave of anger.

'Where have you been? I've been trying and trying…'

'I know, I know.' The high voice was impatient. 'Sorry, darling. I can see loads of missed calls – I'm just working through them now. They take away your mobile at the clinic. They're very strict about it. My shrink say it cancels out all the good the treatment has done.'

Clinic. Shrink. Treatment. Oh, for crying out loud! thought Helen, her blood beginning to boil as she remembered the agonies of anxiety she and her staff had gone through trying and failing to contact Izzy. Searching the park and nearby spinney where Jago had picked up the missing stirrup. Ringing round in wider and wider circles…

She couldn't trust herself to speak as Izzy went on, 'I wanted to tell you I've been balloted out of the Ballymaher championships. They're over-subscribed, so I won't be taking Suleiman over to Co. Louth after all. Disappointing, but there it is, and I'm not sure he is quite ready to compete at that level anyway. So I'll drive down as usual on Monday for a schooling session with Marcus Gibbons – you must have heard of him: former *chef d'équipe* for the Dutch team and very busy, but he's agreed to give me a few lessons, just to put an edge on our performance, and meanwhile…'

Helen stopped listening. 'It's Izzy,' she hissed at Jonah, as he came into the office, shoving Angus and his toy tractor along with his crutch. 'You'd better talk to her before I say something rude.'

He glanced at her puffy, reddened eyes and took the receiver without a word as she scooped up the protesting Angus.

'Potty first, tractor second.'

As she carried him out she heard Jonah's warm, friendly voice: 'My dear girl – where *have* you been? We've got the whole world and his wife looking for you.'

Helen gave him ten minutes to chat her up while she dealt with Angus and repaired her own face. 'Well? Where was she?' she demanded as he rang off.

'Fancied a few days' pampering in an upmarket spa recommended by a friend,' he said with studied neutrality.

'Some people!' It was the nearest she had heard him come to criticising Isabel.

'How much did you tell her?'

'Just what she needed to know. That Suleiman had got out and was a bit scratched, but nothing serious.' He paused and gave her an assessing look before adding. 'I didn't go into the rest of it.'

'Not about…' she began, trying to keep her voice level, but couldn't finish the sentence. Master Mariner had been special, Noel's wedding present to her.

McAndrews the vet had been sympathetic but unequivocal. 'I'm sorry, Helen, but there's really nothing we can do. We can fix that leg up to a point, pump him full of antibiotics and hope no infection sets in, but you have to face it: it would cost you an arm and a leg, and he'd never be really right again. Not to hunt, and with a gelding – well, you don't have many options. Kindest thing is to shoot him right away.'

So she had held Mariner's headcollar and talked to him while he stood on three legs patiently waiting for the sharp crack of the humane killer. And when he had collapsed and the kennelman had attached him to the winch, she had accepted the headcollar and walked back dry-eyed to her car. It was only now, after a sleepless night of memories, that she seemed unable to stop crying.

He had been such a special horse and done so much. Always willing, always trying his best. Bred in France and raced there on the Flat as a two-year-old, then bought as a store by an English trainer. He had won a couple of hurdle races, but wasn't really fast enough, and only showed his real talent over the big regulation fences, when he won and was placed in three-mile chases up and down the country before a fall at Doncaster ended his hopes of racing glory.

Noel had picked him up cheap at Leicester Sales, and slowly introduced him to a new career as a hunter, and a Rolls-Royce of a hunter he had become: beautifully mannered, apparently tireless, and a fearless jumper who always did his best for his rider, whether it was a nervous mum or a dashing young blood at the top of the hunt. Everyone who had ever ridden him loved him.

I should never have hired him out to that old ass of a Colonel, she raged against herself, but the fact remained that Mariner was a surefire moneyspinner whose £200 weekly contribution to the livery business throughout the hunting season could not be ignored.

Yesterday, at his wife's request, she had been to visit the old ass of a Colonel in his hospital bed. She hadn't wanted to, but Dora, with her fuzzy hair and perpetually worried expression was a friend, and she insisted.

'He's been asking for you,' she said. 'Something on his mind, not that he's making a lot of sense, if I'm honest. He wants to apologise.'

'Tell him there's no need. Accidents happen,' said Helen stiffly. 'I'm not much good in hospitals anyway.'

'Oh, please,' Dora pleaded. 'It's all so horrible. There was I, sitting in the pub with a G&T waiting for him to turn up, and some Chink rings my mobile to say he's been found in their school grounds, and would I come quickly because they've sent for an ambulance.'

'How did they get on to you?'

'Grapevine, of course. They rang Marjorie Whittle because she's Hunt secretary, and she remembered hearing Willie fix up a lift home from the pub, so she gave them my number and bingo, there I was. Sitting duck. Oh, do go and put his mind at rest.'

So reluctantly Helen had gone, and been shocked to find the ruddy-faced, confident Colonel yellow and shrunken, head heavily bandaged and arms attached to drips.

'Mrs Murray? He's been asking for you,' the nurse whispered, showing her in. 'Just a few minutes, please. I'm afraid he's very poorly. We don't want to tire him.'

'Hello, Willie,' she said from the door.

No response. It seemed idiotic to ask how he was feeling, but she said it anyway. Again there was no answer.

'Willie,' she said more forcefully. 'It's me. Helen. What did you want to say to me?'

Nothing.

She fidgeted by the bed and looked round for the nurse,

but she had gone. How long was she expected to stay here, talking to an unresponsive patient? She ate a few grapes from a bowl and stared out of the window at a lawn where a dozen fat rabbits were grazing. She was busy. She had a hundred things to do before dark and Gus must be picked up soon or his carer would create.

'Willie!' she said loudly, and at last he opened an eye.

His voice was husky, almost inaudible, but she caught the word 'Sorry.'

'It's OK, Willie.'

'Not OK. Not the horse's fault.'

'No.' Of course it wasn't, you numskull, she raged inwardly. He was just doing what you told him to do. No horse jumps a gate unless the rider makes him do it. It was *your* fault, and poor Mariner paid the price.

Tears welled up in her eyes and she turned towards the door, but Willie was getting agitated, trying to sit up, pulling out the drips. A sinewy brown hand shot out and gripped her wrist before she could snatch it away, and a cannula ripped off. He was struggling with words, but she wasn't interested in what he said. All she wanted was to get out of there.

'Light blinded us. Right in our eyes,' he gulped huskily. 'Couldn't see a thing.'

To her relief the door opened and the nurse bustled in. Clicking her tongue in disapproval, she began settling him down, restoring order. 'Now then, Colonel Marshall, what's all this? Can't have you getting up yet, doctor's orders. You'd better go,' she murmured to Helen, and thankfully she made her escape.

There had been no chance to tell Jonah about her hospital visit because by the time she had finished evening stables a scribbled note on the kitchen table informed her that he had gone out to an emergency meeting of the Hunt Committee.

*Don't wait supper. May be a long session.* It was clear that the Confucius Centre were not going to let matters rest, and if not out for blood, they were bent on compensation for damaged property. Bent, moreover, on reinforcing the message that incursions by the Hunt on to their land were not welcome.

She left cold ham and salad on the table and went to bed without seeing him.

*****

Hardly had Jonah finished talking to Isabel than the phone rang again.

'Thought I'd run the draft of my grovelling letter past you before sending it off,' said Marjorie Whittle, and Jonah sighed.

'OK. Fire away.' He listened, grinning, as she read it out. 'Perfect! Well done! Spot on. The soft answer turneth away wrath, eh?'

'You can't lay it on too thick with these people,' said Marjorie defensively. 'They're incredibly touchy. Shame culture, I know all about it: remember I was brought up in Taiwan. We had to bow to our teachers and I was always in trouble because I was taller than most of them.'

'No, really? Right. You send that off pronto and we'll see if it fixes the problem.' He paused, then said in a different tone, 'One bit of good news: Isabel has agreed to buy two more horses for Fergal. You know he's been beefing all season about being under-horsed, and cursing the Committee for pennypinching? Well, he won't be able to complain about that anymore.'

'That should put a spring in his step. Thank God for Izzy!' exclaimed Marjorie. 'Not good news from the hospital, though. Poor old Willie had a bad night. Between you and me, they think he's not going to make it.'

Helen caught the name and raised her eyebrows interrogatively and he shook his head and gave a thumbs-down. 'Oh, Lord! Poor old sod. Well, we can but hope.'

'Judging by what Dora said this morning, that won't be enough,' said Marjorie soberly.

*****

The Church of St Michael and All Angels was packed for Willie Marshall's funeral a week later. Hunting was suspended as a mark of respect. The organist wove arrangements of 'D'ye Ken John Peel' and 'Drink, Puppy, Drink' into the opening music, to which many mourners could be seen silently mouthing the words, and when the family party retreated to a corner of the churchyard for the interment, Fergal the huntsman, in full livery, blew *Gone to Ground*, following it a moment later with the rousing notes of *Gone Away*.

'A lovely funeral. Perfect. Just what I'd want myself,' was the general verdict, and at the graveside the wall of solid backs of hunt supporting farmers and terriermen which kept both the press and saboteurs at bay came in for particular praise.

'I didn't even ask them to do it,' said Dora tearfully. 'They just formed up and shielded us from any unpleasantness. So tactful.'

Through it all Piers Marshall wandered in a daze, responding politely to expressions of sympathy but allowing his stepmother to make all arrangements. She was a good sort, he acknowledged. She had welcomed him back as if he had never moved out of his father's house in a huff. He had shaved and had his hair cut, and he hadn't been back to Fern's pad: he wasn't sure he wanted ever to see her again. Nevertheless, he knew she and her mates were watching him. That was why they had been hanging about the churchyard during the funeral.

Reuben hadn't waited to check his pictures before sending them to the local press, who had run them with banner headlines, but with the Colonel's death the question of how he had fallen and why had become a subject of intense scrutiny. What had the cameraman been doing there? Even the police were taking an interest. The sabs were afraid Piers would implicate them, but Corky had scared him into silence.

'You never saw that pic of your dad before it turned up in the paper, get it? You don't know who took it or where it was took, or how a camera happened to be there, right?'

'But you said...'

'You listen to what I'm saying *now*.' Corky took Piers by the collar and put his unshaven face so close that Piers could see the yellow roots of his teeth. He smelled feral, and the hard knuckles pressed against his neck were a frightening hint of what might follow.

'Now listen, buster. You dob us in and you're going to know about it. One word from you to the police, or that woman who runs the stable, or your family, and you'll get a kicking you'll never forget. You keeps your mouth shut, young Piers, if you knows what's good for you, and in future you leaves Fern alone. You don't write her no more poems and you don't kip on her settee... She's my girl and not for the likes of you. Understood?'

Half-choked as he was, Piers felt a tiny glow of pride that Corky recognised him as a rival, though at the same time a flicker of resentment pulsed through him. Experience, however, warned him this was no time to push his luck.

'OK,' he muttered, and Corky reinforced his message with a shake that rattled his teeth.

'*Remember!*' he growled, and let him drop to the floor.

There had been times at school when Piers had been goaded into forcefully confronting a bully, and they had never turned out well. He had quickly learnt it was better to keep his head down. To smile. Make a joke of it. Maybe salve his pride later by making up a short, cutting, anonymous verse that would reach his enemy by roundabout ways and could easily be denied.

'Pretend to be thicker than you are,' advised his Gran, who had run a pub and dealt with plenty of bullies herself. People always told you to stand up to them and they would back off, but she found making a bully's friends laugh at him more effective. Piers was a little chap, bespectacled, a swot – a natural target for bullies – so he needed a range of subtler weapons to survive school.

Schooldays were long behind him, but early lessons remained. For a long, frosty week he brooded over how to get even with Corky and at the same time publicise the saboteurs' guilt for his father's death. There was no doubt in his mind that it had been the flash of Reuben's camera that disorientated the horse, fatally arresting his momentum. Why else would Corky have made such a point of telling him to keep his mouth shut?

So what had Reuben been doing in the grounds of the Confucius Centre as dusk was falling? Why were the school's new owners so hostile to the Hunt? Piers could still remember the old Misses Rigby, one scrawny and one fat, but his clearest memory was of the magnificent tea parties they would give to mark the end of term. Then the dining-room table would be so loaded with cakes, scones, sandwiches and every kind of fruit juice that it was difficult to find space for a plate, and the wooden forms that surrounded it were crammed not only with the school's pupils, but every hungry child in the neighbourhood.

'Three cheers for Miss Jane and Miss Brenda!' the head boy or girl would shout as the meal concluded, and the old ladies would simper and wipe away a tear as they thanked their dear pupils for the accolade.

It seemed unlikely that the end-of-term feast was a tradition that survived the change of ownership. What was less clear was why a Confucius Centre should base itself in such a secluded place if its *raison d'être* was, as Google affirmed, the promotion of Chinese culture, languages and way of life. Propaganda on behalf of the Chinese People's Party, in effect. Other European countries banned Confucius Centres. It was only Britain that welcomed the money the Chinese Communist Party lavished on universities and so-called cultural events. Only Britain turned a blind eye to their spying.

Was this what the Misses Rigby's school had become? They would, thought Piers, be mortified. He decided he owed it to them as well as his father do a little research on the subject.

A week of hard frost before Christmas is a blow to any hunt, and a particular nuisance for a livery stable which relies on a small staff. With the ever-present threat of azoturia – a type of paralysis – striking corned-up horses suddenly deprived of exercise, Helen insisted that each of her charges should leave the stable for at least two hours a day, which led to a certain amount of friction between the livery clients who all seemed to want the indoor school at the same time, preferring it to turning their horses out in a New Zealand rug to roll in the muddiest place they could find.

The horse-walker was another option, but a boring and time consuming one: there is always the independent-minded horse who tries to go backwards instead of forwards, refuses to move, or otherwise disrupts what should be a steady progress, and besides, in an unusual mood of thrift, Noel had installed a horse-walker that could take only four at a time.

Helen had an uneasy week keeping the peace between her clients, constantly revising spreadsheets as people telephoned to alter their plans, and the three permanent 'lads', Johnny, Jeremy and Seamus, were kept extra busy mucking out, bringing in supplies of forage, and topping up the straw paths which crisscrossed the yard between the loose boxes and the school.

After the shock of Suleiman's escapade, she had taken to visiting the yard late at night, checking locks and security lights, though Jonah insisted this was unnecessary.

'You'll wear yourself out and then what will I do to replace you?' he said. 'Lightning doesn't strike twice in the same place, you know.'

She had smiled rather wanly. 'I find I can't sleep unless I'm sure everything is OK. Don't worry, it doesn't take long. I'm always in bed by midnight.'

Three nights later, however, when she was standing silently in the feed shed, she caught her breath as she saw a chink of light through the wall of the stallion box and, straining her ears, caught a low murmuring. One voice, or two?

All her fears rushed back. Had the would-be thief returned for another attempt? Was he or she even now quietly putting on saddle and bridle? Had he co-opted Sarah the jenny this time, taken her out of the adjoining stall already to assist with loading the stallion into a waiting lorry? What could she, should she, do?

Paralysed by indecision, she could feel her heart bumping against her ribs as the low murmur was interrupted by the unmistakable *snick!* of a door-bolt drawn back.

'Stop!' she shouted. There was a confused movement inside the stable, a thudding of feet and hoofs, and as she shone her torch at his box a head appeared over the half-door. A human head, a well-known head, blinking and putting up a hand to avoid the beam.

'Jeremy!' she exclaimed. 'What the hell are you doing?'

Smiling sheepishly, Jeremy let himself out of the box, pushing back the stallion who tried to follow.

'It's the tabby's 'ad her kits in his manger, missus. Six on 'em and she won't come out of there. I thought if I moved the lot to Sarah's side there'd be less chance 'e'd trample 'em. Sorry if I give 'ee a fright, missus.'

'Fright! I nearly had a heart attack.'

She drew a deep breath and curbed the instinct to let fly at him. John and Jeremy were the bedrock of her stable staff, not very bright, maybe, but utterly reliable. If either or both of them departed in a huff, she would be sunk. With an effort she forced a laugh and made a joke of it – 'you and your kittens!' – and he advised her to go back to bed and 'stop a-worriting.'

'The trouble is, I can't,' she told Jonah next morning, and he just nodded.

'We've all noticed it. Can't go on – you're wearing yourself out. Now how about asking that father of yours to spend a bit of time with us? Wouldn't that help?' He held up a hand as she began to protest. 'No, let me finish. I know you've had a row – well, a bit more than a row – and you've both said things you probably regret, but isn't it time to call it quits? To mend fences? Your sisters think so, because they've been nagging me to talk to you. To make you see sense, as they put it, because they can't.'

Traitors, she thought fiercely. Sally and even little Marina, going behind her back. Siding with the enemy. How could they? But then, at first neither of them had liked Noel, either, any more than her father did. That was the root of the problem.

'He'll let you down, Helen,' her father had said when she told him their plans. 'I know he's a good-looking bloke and very charming and all that, but it's all surface gloss. I haven't been a policeman for God knows how many years without being able to recognise his type, and I'm not prepared to let my daughter – my darling eldest daughter – marry a man I

don't trust. You've done very well in your Bar exams. You've
got the offer of a pupillage in an excellent Chambers, and the
chance of a good career, and now you're proposing to throw it
all up and marry a horse-dealer. A man I can only describe as a
chancer. An opportunist. A parasite who lives off his brother,
with no prospects, no profession...'

'Stop,' Helen had said through stiff lips. 'You've said
enough. I don't want to hear any more.'

But her father continued as if she had not spoken. 'I mean
it, darling. Please listen to me, and think what your mother
would have wanted. We all make mistakes: I don't blame you
for being carried away. As I said, he's a very charming fellow.
I don't even mind about the baby. It's not the best of starts for
the poor little beggar, but we'll all help you.' He had smiled.
'Family help goes a long way, you know.'

Helen had said fiercely, 'I don't want your help, Dad, or
your advice. I love Noel and I'm going to marry him, and you
can't stop me. This is my life, and you can just keep out of it.'

That anger had supported her through the following
months, and both her father and sisters had attended the
registry office wedding, though the tension between her family
and Noel's was palpable. It didn't help when Noel's ex-wife
insisted on being there; and though Jonah, the peace-maker,
did his best to smooth everyone's feelings at the luncheon he'd
arranged, Helen was glad when their guests made excuses and
left early.

Her father had been stony-faced throughout, and both her
sisters close to tears. 'Don't worry, darling. They'll get over it,'
said Noel, hugging her. 'When they see how happy we are,
and what a success we make of this business, they'll forget that
they ever tried to stop us marrying.'

And they had been happy. For nearly two years they had
been as entirely happy as any married couple could be.

Noel always looked on the bright side. His glass was perpetually half-full, his optimism infectious. He loved fast cars and starred restaurants and the worlds of fashion and celebrity. Most of all he loved trading in horses, the infinite variety of bloodstock sales and the wheeling and dealing that accompanied them. He knew everyone who was anyone in the horse world, and would have spent their annual budget fifty times over if Jonah, the self-declared bean-counter, had not put a brake on him. When he sold a horse, he would usually buy two replacements, and it was over a year before Helen began to wonder if the plates he was spinning so blithely were kept aloft by anything but faith.

'Nothing venture, nothing gain, darling,' he would say when she questioned if they could afford some new acquisition who would need two years' growing time before they could expect any return on his purchase price. 'You've got to spot potential, and that, though I say it myself, is my speciality. With bloodstock you have to take breeding into account, and be prepared to be patient. It's no good expecting miracles overnight. Jonah understands that.'

She had to admit that he had some spectacular successes, building up weedy yearlings and selling them to Arabs as handsome, two-year-old sprinters, but equally often he would decide that the hoped-for potential was never going to manifest itself, and the animal in question would be quietly sold as a hunter, hack, or for peanuts as a 'fun horse' to some obsessed teenager.

'Amazing what the Bank of Mum and Dad will shell out to keep their little darling happy,' he said one day, showing her a cheque as the tail-light of a trailer past its best vanished down the drive.

Helen was horrified. 'You can't have sold them the Perseus filly! She's not sound.'

'Look, my angel,' he said, pulling her close and stroking her hair, 'when a girl falls in love with a horse, the best thing is to let her have it. I can guarantee that filly will have a blissful life being petted and cared for by that sweet girl, and if she's not up to being ridden – well, veterinary science gets better all the time...'

'That's immoral!' she'd said, pulling away.

'Come on, grow up. What do you think 'fun horse' means? And *caveat emptor*, come to that. If you want the stables full of *bouches inutiles*, I certainly don't, and I'm prepared to do something about it.'

She knew that was a covert dig at her for keeping five hunters in all winter, but since they spent the summer at grass and each brought in the best part of £100 every time she hired them out she had no intention of cutting back this modest source of income.

Bean-counting Jonah encouraged her, and since the whole estate belonged to him, she felt secure in maintaining her stance.

'My brother has big ideas,' he explained, 'and when he makes a killing, it tends to be one that will keep the wolves from the door for a good long time. That's why I give him his head...within reason. But now and again he gets things wrong, so we have to budget for that, too.'

His battered, slightly lopsided face, its expression so different from Noel's easygoing confident charm, broke into a smile.

'As you may have noticed, I'm the cautious type myself when it comes to money, and I like to keep the books balanced.'

She had indeed noticed. No two brothers were ever more different – perhaps that was why they got on so well, she thought. Jonah ran the farm, managed the accounts, and lived

– or rather rattled around in – the main house, fending off the attempts of motherly women who would have liked to share it with him.

Noel's smart London house had been a casualty of divorce, but he made the best of it, renting a two-bed apartment in the Paddington Basin for those nights when travel or business dinners kept him in town.

'It's fairly crummy, but really all I need. Just somewhere to lay my head if the plane's late or I've drunk too much to drive,' he said, laughing, and Helen herself found it a useful place to dump parcels on her occasional shopping sprees to London which, after Gus was born, became ever more rare.

The substantial front lodge, however, built for a gatekeeper with many children, was a charming folly with wide views of the park on one side and the avenue of chestnut trees on the other. Just a couple of minutes' walk from the main house and the same from the imposing archway leading to the stable yard, it had been inherited by Noel as his share of the estate and, after the collapse of his first marriage, became his permanent home.

Cottages dotted about the park and village housed other members of the staff: Seamus and his wife occupied a converted barn, while the twins Jeremy and John Conisby lived rent-free in the back-drive gatehouse.

The deep freeze in relations between Helen and her family slowly thawed. Emails proved the thin end of the wedge, then both Sally and Marina had sent birthday cards, followed by a rather stiff letter of congratulation from her father when Angus was born. She knew he still regretted the legal career she had thrown away, and thought her a fool for settling for life with a twice-married man, looking after other people's horses, but even he was not completely immune to Noel's charm and good nature when he had driven Marina over to visit her sister for the autumn half-term week, which happened to coincide with the Opening Meet of the West Layton Hounds.

Marina was very slight so Helen put her up on the calmer of Candy Cutler's show-jumping ponies, and she returned ecstatic, splattered with mud from head to heel, and wildly enamoured of her brother-in-law.

'Noel told me to stick to his tail wherever he went, so I did, and we galloped and galloped and jumped enormous fences which most of the horses refused. It was amazing. We even had to swim a river, and at the end there were only six of us left. Oh, why can't I stay here and hunt all winter instead of going back to school?'

Helen had looked inquiringly at her husband, who laughed. 'It's true enough. We had to ford the Carling Brook but there was so much water that Little Orchid was practically afloat. Yes, we had a good day. You mustn't imagine it's always like that, Marina. Sometimes we just tootle about the woods all day and everyone gets bored stiff.'

This was an exaggeration because Noel himself was never bored. Good-looking, self-assured, a natural athlete, he was a favourite wherever he went, and his fan club encompassed ladies of all ages, sporting and unsporting, rich and poor. Good for trade, Helen assured herself. Safety in numbers, though it was difficult not to feel a twinge of jealousy when she watched his eyes linger on some beauty at a race meeting, and saw how the beauty herself reacted to that look, preening as he put a hand on her arm, or fought his way to the bar to fetch her a drink.

He smiled when she admitted this, and shook his head. 'Oh, my love! So the green-eyed monster has been getting at you, and I never noticed. I'm so sorry! Poor Prue simply couldn't bear it. She didn't understand that it's all an act. Part of the job,' He hugged her to him. 'You do see that, don't you?

It's the way the business works: I'm the front man; I bring in the customers, but without Jonah to crunch the numbers and you to keep the machine running, I'd be useless.'

So his ex-wife had reacted as she had. She felt a flicker of fellow feeling for 'poor Prue'. She said, 'If it's an act, it's a very convincing one. You certainly had me fooled,' and thought he looked relieved.

'You must remember I've had years of practice.'

Shows, sales, races: the horse world is always travelling, and Noel went with it, the pages of his passport crowded with stamps of different nations, the top of his desk overflowing with programmes and schedules of forthcoming events all over the world.

Dark-eyed veiled beauties and assertive cosmopolitan millionairesses might throng Helen's dreams, but in daylight she kept them at bay with the constant activity of a livery stable which, as always when people and horses are involved, brought its own share of problems, dramas, and crises.

'Think about it,' advised Jonah, as he saw her instinctive rejection of his suggestion to ask her father for help. 'He'd probably welcome the chance to get to know his grandson.'

'OK,' she agreed without marked enthusiasm, but a chance encounter with Piers Marshall made her change her mind.

After prolonged thought, Piers had decided that the best way to approach her would be in the woods, rather than risking anyone seeing him going into the stable yard and word of it getting back to Fern via her brother Jago, who was always hanging about the stables helping Candy Cutler with her ponies. A longstanding but neglected invitation from Jonah Murray to thin out the pigeons feasting on his kale would give him the excuse to intercept Helen when she went for a hack, or took the horses out to grass, and barely had this plan formed in his mind than the perfect opportunity presented itself.

'Hang on. I'll open that for you,' he offered, gun on shoulder, as she approached the gate to the railed paddock one windy afternoon, her hands fully occupied with the halter-ropes of three horses who were keen to get their heads down.

'Oh…thanks.'

He let them through, and watched as she slipped off the headcollars and let them canter away, nipping each other and bucking to get their blood moving before settling down to graze.

'Piers?' she said tentatively, looking at him properly for the first time, taking in the gun, camo smock, the game-bag, the spaniel. 'Sorry, I hardly recognised you. It's – it's been ages since we met. Have you been having a go at the pigeons? Jonah will be pleased. I'm so sorry about your father.'

'Yes.' He braced himself. 'Actually that's what I want to talk to you about. My stepmum said you'd been to see him in hospital just before he died.' He stopped, unsure how to go on.

'Yes.'

Piers said in a rush, 'Did he say anything about being dazzled by a light, just as the horse was jumping?'

Helen frowned, remembering the hospital bed, the scrawny hand gripping her wrist. 'Yes. He told me the light blinded him. The photograph was in the papers. Unattributed. You must have seen it.'

'That's what I wanted to tell you. It was taken by one of the sabs – you know, hunt saboteurs – who want to get hunting banned completely.'

'How do you know?'

'Because they showed it to me – before sending it to the press. Boasting that some old geezer – meaning Dad – had come a cropper.'

'Why show *you*?'

Piers looked at his boots, his cheeks aflame. 'Because they

thought I was one of them. Well, I was, in a way. Then.'

'And now you've changed your mind?' she said coldly.

'Sorry, Piers. Your so-called *friends* caused the death of my best horse, and I just don't want to talk about it.' She turned away, but he caught at her arm.

'And my father, don't forget.'

'Your father did something stupid and brought it on himself. Now let me go. I'm busy, even if you aren't.'

He said desperately, 'Wait, you haven't heard it all. You know Jago Smith?'

Her steps slowed. 'Of course I do. He's got a job at that Chinese school. Groundsman, I think. He's a bit of a pest, to be honest, because he comes over here after work and hangs about saying he's helping Candy, though she can manage those ponies quite well by herself. What's he got to do with it?'

'Well, his sister's called Fern…'

'I know Fern. She cuts my hair.'

Piers said awkwardly, 'She was my – well – kind of girlfriend, and she organises the hunt saboteurs.'

'Are you sure? She's doesn't look as if she could run to save her life. And she's never said anything about it to me.' She stared at him for a moment, then said vigorously, 'If she is, that's the last time she'll be cutting my hair. All right, go on. So she's your girlfriend?'

'No. After Dad's…accident, we split up. Now she's with another sab called Corky, and they say if I tell anyone who took that photograph they'll give me a kicking I won't forget.'

Thin, pale, bespectacled: he looked as if one kick would be enough to flatten him, but there was a set to his jaw which reminded her powerfully of his father. 'So why are you telling me?' she asked. 'Do you *want* them to kick you?'

'I want to warn you. They're not a joke. They're violent.' He paused, then said in a rush, 'Jago or his mate Reuben took that photograph. Like you say, he's always over here, hanging around the stables. Listening. Anything he hears he passes on to Fern, and she briefs the sabs.'

'Oh, he does, does he? That's interesting.'

He nodded.

Helen said, 'Thanks for telling me. We've been wondering where they got their information on where the hunt is meeting. I'll warn Fergal – in fact I'd better tell the Hunt Committee – but I'll make sure to keep you out of it.'

'OK.' He glanced at the sky where a few birds were commuting between the wood and the field of kale. 'Better get back to the pigeons. Don't want to be seen talking to you...' He whistled and the spaniel was at his heels in an instant.

She watched him climb the fence and slip back into the rustling wet leaves, disappearing beneath the branches of the hide as a rabbit vanishes into a bramble bush.

*****

Before starting the Ford Fiesta, Anne Cutler surveyed her reflection in the rear-view mirror, then leant forward to pluck a single white hair from among her dark curls. One that Fern missed, she thought, examining it; she really is a pretty useless hairdresser. Why can't I afford to go to a proper salon? Why can't I afford any of the things I want? Why do I have to toil away at this dead-end job and take all the risk while William has all the excitement? Money doesn't matter to him because he's never had any, but for me...

For a moment she allowed herself to daydream about what life had been like before the police and the press came knocking and took Daddy away for questioning. She had been twelve then, and Prue fifteen; the Cutler sisters whom everyone envied because they were pretty and clever and rich, and their ponies won every show they entered. Well, most people envied them. Others called them pot-hunters, and said the ponies were looked after and schooled by grooms, and Prue and Anne only rode them in the show-ring.

From the distance of twenty years, Anne had to admit there was a certain amount of truth in this. Daddy hadn't wanted his daughters to muck out stables or clean saddlery; he'd said, 'That's the grooms' job. Why keep a dog and bark yourself?' So now that Anne had a daughter of her own and there was neither money nor a groom, she was obliged to accept Jago Smith's offer to help with Candy's two ponies, and keep them at livery in Jonah Murray's Barleycourt yard.

At the time it seemed to her to be a good solution. Jago was willing to augment his wages, and she had little time to spare. From odd remarks, however, she sensed that he was not much liked by regular Barleycourt personnel, accused of hanging around, borrowing other people's clippers and lead-ropes, and other unspecified crimes against efficient stable management.

It helped, of course, that Jonah had once been almost a relation – how did you describe the brother of your brother-in-law? – and he was not the kind of person who would cut off a relationship just because the marriage had come unstuck. Anne suspected that he deliberately tempered the wind to the shorn lamb by charging her less for the ponies' upkeep than any other owner would have paid, but everything to do with horses – shoes, saddlery, transport – is expensive and, with only her salary from the Confucius Centre to rely on, even Jonah's modest monthly charges still left her chronically short of money.

A movement caught by the rear-view mirror warned her that Mr Li, her supervisor, was watching the car from his office, wondering why she hadn't driven away, and she hastily started the engine. The Chinese were a suspicious lot and, working behind the scenes, William Yu had been obliged to pull a good many strings both here and in Hong Kong before she was taken on. The last thing she – and he – wanted was for her to lose her job. Now, she thought, they had accepted her and her carefully edited back-story, composed, checked and double-checked by William and his dissident friends so convincingly that sometimes she even believed in it herself.

According to this scenario, she was the innocent, rather stupid daughter of a disgraced English businessman; given work at a no-count office job by a benevolent uncle in Hong Kong; fell for the high-living scion of a Party official – a 'little emperor' as he and his like were known, handsome, educated, rich and open-handed – and fell pregnant; abandoned by lover at his family's insistence; returned to England to lick her wounds and raise her daughter as a struggling single mum, chronically short of money and looking to capitalise on her knowledge of Chinese.

Well, the last part was true enough, and her new employers seemed to have swallowed the rest. Sometimes she would feel a thrill of satisfaction that she was delivering even the smallest tweak to the tail of the cruel regime that had cost William and his family so much: at others times she shivered at the thought of what they would do to him if they caught him. Nothing would please them more than to lay hands on counter-propagandist in chief and constant thorn in their flesh William Yu.

For two years now he had been in hiding, occasionally surfacing from mysterious visits to the States or Taiwan about which she knew better than to question him.

'If you don't know, you can't tell, ' he pointed out reasonably. 'Concentrate on living your back story until it seems more real than the truth,' and because she feared for his safety, she obeyed to the letter, renting the caretaker's isolated cottage from the Centre, and only venting her frustration at her lack of money with her sister Prudence, a big spender herself who was always up to her ears in debt.

'You'll have to borrow,' said Prue briskly.

'But what about paying it back?'

'That's no big deal. Do it in stages, a bit at a time.'

Anne had been doubtful. 'The bank knows exactly what I earn...'

'Heavens! I'm not suggesting you borrow from the bank. Try one of your friends, you'll get much better terms.' A thought struck her. 'Try your employers. They're absolutely rolling. Ask them for a temporary loan – call it a soft loan – and make it a big one, so they know you're serious. It's no good fiddling about with small amounts. Try it, darling. After all, they can always say no.'

So Anne had summoned up courage to ask for ten thousand pounds from her supervisor, and tried to hide her astonishment when he agreed without question.

'You will pay us back when your ship comes in,' he said with the ingratiating smile which reminded her of a well-fed cat. 'Are you sure that is all you need?'

She assured him it was, then wished she had asked for twice as much. Prue was right. A discreet private loan was far less hassle than borrowing from the bank. Two thoughts had to be pushed to the back of her mind: firstly how to pay back the money, and secondly the certainty that William Yu would not approve. Well, he need never know. His lack of interest in her finances had often irritated her, but in this instance it would be a bonus. She would buy the promising show-jumping ponies which Candy coveted and Noel told her were a snip at £4,000 apiece – 'win a few rosettes and find the right buyer and you could double your money overnight,' – and not have to worry about her overdraft for months to come.

The first part of this plan had gone swimmingly. Little Orchid, the 12hh. strawberry roan with the pretty neat-muzzled head and spring-heels of a true Welsh Mountain pony, and Fireball, 14hh. of jet-propelled palomino, were indeed stars in the making, and quickly justified Noel's opinion by winning or being placed in every local competition.

Much less easy was getting Candy to part with either of them when the Chinese began to ask for their money back.

'They're *mine*, Mum! You gave them to me. You can't just take away a present. I've entered them for...' and she reeled off a list of engagements at indoor shows that covered the weekends of the whole of the winter months then, pre-empting her mother's most likely objection, 'and if you don't want to drive me there and hang about waiting all day, Jago says he'll be glad to take us.'

Which was the last thing Anne wanted. So she said briskly, 'Nonsense, darling. You know I love seeing you compete. Of course I'll drive you to shows,' while thinking to herself that the Confucius Centre would just have to wait for its money.

It was true that few things gave her more pleasure than seeing Candy on the turbo-charged Fireball or careful, steady Little Orchid beat off the opposition with two clear rounds and a jump-off, then fly round the arena in a lap of honour, her grin lighting up the gloomiest day and compensating for the damp, chilly hours of waiting for her class. Anne remembered so well the thrill she had felt herself when the judge had called her into the middle of the show-ring and, after nail-biting minutes of suspense, placed her pony at the top of the line – ahead of Isabel Garraway. Old rivalries died hard.

So when in early December her supervisor Mr Li, with great politeness, asked if she yet felt able to repay the small loan he had extended, she answered blandly that she hoped to be in a better position to do so at the end of the year, when certain negotiations had been concluded, and Mr Li nodded understanding.

'Ah! Negotiations!' He savoured the word as if it was a particularly juicy sea-slug. 'So many negotiations to buy good horses.'

Who had told him she was buying horses with his money? Jago, of course, the blabbermouth. The thought of him discussing her affairs with Mr Li was distasteful. She said stiffly, 'My former brother-in-law is an expert. I rely on his advice.'

'Ah, that is good. He helps you with negotiations.' The way he said it sounded faintly obscene, as if she was admitting an affair with Noel.

'After negotiations finished, you repay our loan? Maybe one month or two?'

'Of course,' she said, smiling, though her heart sank as a definite date was proposed. 'In the New Year – how about that?'

'New Year. Very good,' agreed Mr Li.

Anne was worried enough to ring Noel Murray that evening when she got home and found him – for a wonder – not only in the country but preparing to take his wife out for a celebratory birthday dinner.

'Why don't you join us?' he said in his friendly expansive way. 'We see so little of you nowadays. Either you're slogging away at that Chinese school or I'm abroad.'

'No, no,' she said, laughing and thinking that in Helen's place she would be horrified at the suggestion of a gooseberry at their romantic dinner. 'I just wanted your advice about something. Have you a moment?'

'Always ready with advice, though no guarantees how good it will be.'

Over the line she heard the squeak of a cork being eased from a bottle. 'OK, fire away. What's the problem?'

'I'm thinking of selling Little Orchid – you know, the roan pony – and wondered if you could find me a buyer?'

'Hang on, Annie. Are you sure you want to do that?' She sensed disapproval. 'He's a really good pony and gets on well with your daughter. Frankly, I think you'll find him difficult to replace.'

'I'm not thinking of replacing him. Candy doesn't need two ponies and, to be honest, I need the money.'

'Hmm...' She could almost see him turning it over in his mind, considering the options. After a moment's silence he said, 'Well, I could of course find someone to pay a decent price, but I still think it's a bad idea. Ponies like him don't grow on trees, and he's only – what? Six? Seven? Best years of his life still in front of him. You've done all the hard work, got him going well: now why not take advantage of that and let your daughter have a little fun with him?'

Again he paused, then added, 'Tell you what, Annie: let me lend you whatever you need and...'

'No!' she interrupted more forcefully than she meant to. 'It's sweet of you even to suggest it, but I wouldn't dream of letting you bail me out. The way Candy's growing, her feet will soon be touching the ground on Little Orchid: that's why I'm thinking of selling him.'

'So you'll change your mind?'

She summoned a laugh. 'With you and Candy ganging up on me, what else can I do?'

So bang goes another money-making scheme, she thought resignedly, putting down the receiver. Noel was a dear, but she really couldn't borrow from him, no matter how much Prue urged her to. In any case, since the humiliating failure of their last moneymaking plan, which had left her sister with scraped ribs and a sprained ankle, Anne felt disinclined to propose wild plans involving horses…

Kidnapping Suleiman from his stable, hiding him a hundred miles away and demanding a ransom which would pay off their debts had been Anne's own idea, and after initial reluctance Prue had agreed to help her.

'Don't forget he's a stallion. Are you sure you can manage him?' she'd asked, but Anne had no doubts.

'No problem – he's very well-mannered. Everyone says so. If a wimp like Isabel can ride him, there's no reason to think he'll be too much for me,' she'd said with a laugh.

'Maybe, but you'd better let me ride him. How long is it since you got on a horse?'

'Well, OK. but really, I don't think there'll be any problem. After all, he's travelled all over the world. He probably looks on a trailer as his second home.'

Neither of them remembered the importance of Sarah, the donkey, in getting Suleiman to load, and both were taken by surprise when the stallion reared and refused to go forward as soon as he saw the empty trailer. He spun round like a dancer, gave two enormous bucks which threw Prue's balance and snatched the reins from her hands, and took off along the woodland track as if the hounds of hell were after him.

Anne had raced in pursuit. She just glimpsed an explosion of twigs and a fountain of water as they failed to take the sharp bend round a small pond, and that was where she finally discovered her sister, groaning and gasping as she dragged herself out of the slimy mud and back to solid ground, laughing hysterically.

'Whoops! Never been so fast in my life! Nought to sixty in two seconds flat. A kick in the kidneys and he was away. Yuk! That tastes disgusting.' She spat out a greenish mouthful and croaked,' Come on, we'd best make tracks before that horse wakes everyone in the neighbourhood. We don't want them to find us here.'

Limping and bedraggled, they hurried back to the trailer, heaved up the ramp and drove away. It had not been their finest hour.

Few things keep you awake more surely than worrying about money. Anne spent the next nights tossing restlessly, listening to Candy's even breathing, and devising ever wilder schemes for repairing her finances. She was nearly at the point of admitting she would, after all, have to accept Noel's offer when to her surprise he rang her at work.

'Hey, Annie – good news! I've got you a deal – that is, if you're still set on selling the roan pony?'

'It's not that I want to, but I think I'll have to.' She spoke quietly, conscious that across the room Mr Li had raised his head to listen. 'Look, can I ring you back in a moment?'

He picked up the inference at once, 'Course you can. Sorry to ring you at work, but the chap wants an answer at once because he's on his way to look at something else.'

'Two minutes, then.'

She muttered an excuse to Mr Li and ran out to her car. 'Noel? Sorry about that, but there was someone close to my desk. You said something about a deal?'

'There's a man I know slightly staying here who's been searching high and low for a pony like yours. His son is eight, rides well, but had a fright with a pony that was too strong for him. Now he needs a confidence-giver. A real point-and-click that he can trust to jump when he asks it to and not refuse or take off with him. Struck me that your little roan answers that description.'

He gave her a moment to think it over but her heart had leapt. Now it would only be a question of persuading Candy… She said cautiously, 'What would he pay?' and he laughed.

'Oh, I'll be losing my touch if I don't get him up to six-five, possibly seven.'

'Seven thousand?'

He said deprecatingly, 'I know it's not quite double what you gave for him, but when boys grow they have a habit of growing fast – so I think in the circs it's a fair price.'

'Noel, you're a star. I could hug you.'

'Be my guest.' A chuckle. 'Better tell the Boss first or she might knock you for six. Right, then: that's settled. You get back to work, and have a word with your daughter this evening. All being well, I'll bring Moncrieffe and his nipper over to Barleycourt on Saturday morning for a trial, so mind that pony's looking his best.'

'But wait a mo...' Things were going too fast, getting out of control. 'Candy's at school tomorrow, and I'll have to work.'

'Don't worry, Helen and I will handle it. I'll ring you to say what the deal is and, if you agree, the sale can go through our books as usual and I'll give you the cash next time I see you. How does that sound to you?'

He rang off, and she let out her breath in a whoosh of relief. In the space of a minute or two all her worries had vanished and the world looked a brighter place.

'Your negotiations go well?' said Mr Li solicitously as she re-entered the office.

'Yes, thank you.'

'Good. Then you pay us back in New Year.'

'Of course.' With seven thousand pounds as good as in her pocket, she could afford to give him a smile.

# CHAPTER THREE

'SOMEONE AT THE door, Mum,' called Candy, as her mother was sleepily filling sandwiches for tomorrow's lunchbox.

'Coming!' She dropped the buttery knife and wiped her hands. 'Go to bed,' she hissed at her daughter. 'He'll come up to see you later.'

There was only one person likely to be ringing the bell of this tucked-away cottage at eleven at night. Sure enough, there on the threshold stood William Yu, tired but smiling, almost unrecognisable in an over-large Barbour and wide-brimmed hat from which water dripped in a steady stream. He was tall for a Chinese man, and thinner than when she saw him last, but his dark eyes lit up with pleasure on seeing her.

'What a night! I feared you would be already in bed and I should have to break in.'

'Why didn't you let me know you were coming?' She led him indoors. 'Are you hungry?'

'Starving. The food on the plane was beyond filthy.'

'Plane?'

'From Manchester. Domestic flight. Now no more questions.' He sat at the kitchen table, watching silently as she heated congee, throwing handfuls of raisins, mushrooms, and shreds of ginger into the steaming bowl, which he shovelled in with grunts of pleasure. He sat back at last, ready to describe his latest escape from the black-helmeted thugs who guarded the Manchester consulate.

'They tried to drag me into the compound, but all they got for their trouble was my oldest coat. Like a snake shedding its skin, I left them to enjoy it.'

Anne dreaded these close encounters, which sometimes left him beaten and bruised, but William seemed to revel in them.

'We've a big demo planned for next week, outside the Embassy this time, so there will be banner headlines.'

'Must you go?' she asked, and he looked surprised.

'Certainly I must. It is our best chance to force the Government to ban these pernicious Centres of propaganda, and I need to know who has been sent to orchestrate their response. We must always be one step ahead. Now tell me who has arrived lately in your office, and who has been replaced?'

Write nothing, photograph nothing, entrust nothing to electronic communication – those were the rules by which William had managed to evade his pursuers for years. Chinese expertise in artificial intelligence had grown exponentially in the past decade and since it was no longer safe to store data on burner phones, word of mouth remained the only sure way to share information. Anne had a quick clear memory for faces and a good ear for Chinese names.

Rapidly she listed all the comings and goings of lecturers and visitors over the past month, and he grunted approval. 'Good. Very good. As I thought, they are calling up their big guns to be ready for us. You are a great help to me, Anne.'

Praise from him was so rare that she risked saying, 'So you didn't come to see me tonight?'

His eyes crinkled into half-moons. 'That too. Also to see my daughter.'

'So you've remembered you have a daughter?' she couldn't help saying, but with William any attempt at irony was water off a duck's back. She added, 'She's growing up fast. Don't you think it's time we told her who 'Uncle Will' really is? It's bound to be a shock.'

'No way.' He was emphatic. 'To tell her would endanger you both. Like this you are safe, and while you arrange lectures and Open Days to keep the CCP happy, I can continue my work against them without worrying that they will connect us. Candy is still a child and cannot guard her tongue. We should not ask her to – not yet.'

Reluctantly she nodded. He was right, of course: Candy was a chatterbox, ready to bare her soul to anyone who would listen. She thought of Jago's flapping ears and Mr Li's interest in her financial 'negotiations', and wondered if she herself was becoming paranoid. Living a lie – or even a half-truth – was a strain.

He had brought her two bottles of rice wine, produced from the capacious pockets of his Barbour, and under its cheerful influence their mood lightened. Whatever the restrictions of her present life, they were nothing compared to those Will's father and brothers had to endure in Hong Kong – house arrest, businesses snatched away, beating and imprisonment for anyone who dared to protest – and above all the sense of betrayal as the freedoms enjoyed before the British flag was hauled down were systematically eroded.

In comparison her own gripes seemed very small potatoes indeed.

*****

Barney Moncrieffe's small pale face was almost eclipsed by his crash helmet, but as he pulled up after completing his trial with a flying circuit of fences in the indoor arena, his smile was radiant.

'Wow!' he said, and leaned forward to bury his face in Little Orchid's mane.

Helen and Noel looked at one another and nodded, and Barney's father walked rapidly down from the viewing gallery to join him on the tan.

'I guess Anne can name her price,' said Noel quietly.

'I still think she's mad to sell him. He suits Candy perfectly.'

Noel nodded. 'As a matter of fact, so do I, but when I realised how desperate she is for money I thought the best thing I could do was find him a good home and get her a decent deal.'

'Not because you so love horse-dealing?' teased Helen and he grinned.

'How well you know me, my love! Now watch, listen, and learn while I go to work. I think that little pony has got Charles hooked and he'll happily pay over the odds for him.'

'There's many a slip,' cautioned Helen, but she was wrong. Charles Moncrieffe had made up his mind and a detail like price wasn't going to stop him. After the briefest of conversations the men settled on eight thousand and shook hands. 'I'll get my vet to give him the once-over tomorrow morning, but that should be just a formality,' said Moncrieffe. 'Then if it's OK with you, we'll come and fetch him early in the afternoon, two-ish, so that he has time to settle before Barney goes back to school. Do you mind parting with his outdoor rug as well? We haven't got anything that won't swamp him.'

'We'll throw it in with the rest of his tack,' offered Noel before Helen could answer. 'You might as well start with everything that fits. He's a good pony, Charles, registered Welsh Mountain Section A, and I wish you the best of luck with him. Well done, Barney. You ride him just the way he likes, plenty of leg and no hanging on to his head. You make a good team.'

The boy flushed at the compliment, and covered his confusion by carefully smoothing Little Orchid's mane over to the right side.

'He's lovely,' he muttered.

The men strolled away. 'I'll help you unsaddle him,' Helen offered, but Barney shook his head.

'I'd like to do it myself. If you don't mind,' he added, belatedly remembering his manners.

'Oh, OK. Then I'll show you which is his stable.' That looks like a marriage made in heaven, she thought. There remained only one disturbing niggle.

*****

When Candy saw the motorbike revving gently beside the bus stop, she left her friends and ran over to it.

'Give me a lift, Jago!'

'What'll your ma say?'

'She won't know.' She unclipped the spare helmet and crammed it on, waving an airy hand at her friends and urging, 'Go, go, go!'

'Hold tight, then.' He took off with a roar that left the other children open-mouthed, sending a spray of mud into the side of the school bus, and Candy sighed ecstatically. This was the life!

All too soon he braked to a stop and reluctantly she got off the pillion.

'Help me get the ponies in?' she asked hopefully.

'Nah. Got work to do tonight.' He saw her disappointment and added, 'Your ma going to buy you another pony, then?'

'What do you mean?' Candy gaped at him, astonished.

'Sold the little un this morning, didn't she? Got a good price too, so I hear. Mr Murray fixed it up; all done and dusted by half-ten.'

Candy's mouth was dry. She struggled to speak. 'But – but she can't have.'

'Well, she has. Bloke came with a lorry and fetched him round about three, said he wanted to get him home in daylight. D'you mean she didn't tell you?'

She didn't answer but spun on her heel and ran down the path towards the cottage with tears pouring down her face. Jago watched her go, then kickstarted the bike and set off back the way he had come. He had news for Mr Li which might bring in rather more than a fox-skin.

Keep an eye on that child, Mr Li had instructed him, after paying for half a dozen raw pelts. Get to know her. I think in time she may lead us somewhere interesting.

With that in mind, Jago had made himself useful where he could that winter, carrying haynets and breaking ice on the water trough when there was a hard frost, or bringing Candy's ponies in from the field when she missed the school bus. He seldom spoke to her mother, though instinct told him she would not approve of her daughter riding pillion on his muddy Kawasaki, but on night prowls round his preferred reservoir of foxes he often glimpsed her through the window of the caretaker's cottage.

In pouring rain, he had watched William Yu approach the back door late enough at night for him to report the visit to Mr Li, who received the news with outward impassivity, but thereafter became very busy on his encrypted mobile.

'*Most Urgent. Hidden dragon moving,*' he tapped rapidly.

'*Follow golden oriole to assignation site and destroy*,' and he signed it with the symbol used only by the most elite cadres in the CCP.

*****

'For heaven's sake, darling, what's the matter?' exclaimed Anne as Candy burst through the door, hair dishevelled and tears on her cheeks.

'Jago says you've sold Little Orchid,' she sobbed.

Damn that fellow! thought Anne, who had hoped to have this conversation calmly, at a time of her own choosing.

'Oh, please say it isn't true!'

'Now listen, darling…'

'Oh, then it *is* true. I can't believe it. You're a cruel beast and I hate you. I wish you weren't my mother,' shouted Candy.

'Don't be silly, darling. He's gone to a very good home and you were too big for him anyway.'

Anne's very calmness seemed to infuriate Candy more. She upended her soup bowl on to the tablecloth and banged it with her spoon. 'I wasn't! That's rubbish. You said yourself he could carry two of me, but you don't care about me. All you wanted was to make money out of him. That's all you ever think about, how to get more money!'

This was uncomfortably close to the truth.

Candy ranted on, 'You told me you wouldn't sell Little Orchid without telling me, but that's exactly what you've done. I can't trust anything you say. You told me you'd send Uncle William up to see me last night…'

'Leave Uncle William out of it,' said Anne sharply.

'Why should I? He's my godfather. Why shouldn't I see him? What's so secret that I can't even mention his name?'

'You were asleep.'

'No, I wasn't. I listened to everything you said.'

'What did you hear?'

Anne was seriously alarmed, but her daughter shrugged and said, 'Oh, just a lot of boring rubbish about people at your school. Nothing about selling Little Orchid. Then he went away and didn't even *try* to come up and see me. I hate you and I'll never speak to you again. I wish I was dead.'

\*\*\*\*\*

Bright lights, snowy tablecloths, a glitter of glasses: after the dark wet car park and driving rain, the dining room of The Duke's Arms looked a vision of comfort and civilisation.

'Wonderful to see you, Annie,' said Noel, coming forward to meet her even before the doorman could take her wet coat. 'My poor pet, you're sopping. What a brute I am to bring you out on a night like this.'

He hugged her warmly, then stepped back to admire her carefully assembled glamour, velvet jacket and pants in a flattering vivid green, white trainers secretly borrowed from Candy, whose feet were almost the same size, earrings. 'You're looking wonderful. That colour really suits you.'

Anne's felt her cheeks glow. How different, she could not help thinking, from William Yu and his brusque acceptance of her as a mere domestic chattel, the provider of food and safety whenever he should need it. An underling. No matter that she knew Noel would say the same to any woman, his open admiration filled her with confidence.

'*Flatteur!*' she smiled, then, spotting the champagne bottle on the table behind him, she raised a flirtatious eyebrow: 'Party time?'

'I thought a little celebration was in order.' He signalled to the waiter, who filled their glasses. 'Here's to Barney

Moncrieffe and Little Orchid! May they sweep the board in every competition they enter!' They drank, and he added in a different tone, 'How did your daughter take it, by the way?'

'Not well.' Anne grimaced. The champagne suddenly tasted sour. 'That wretched Jago Smith went and blurted it out to her before I'd had a chance to – well – to warn her. To soften the blow.'

She took another larger sip and some of the glow returned. Candy had seen sense in the end, but she had refused her supper saying she wasn't hungry and avoided a goodnight kiss. There had also been an unacknowledged understanding that some time in the future, if she worked hard and achieved good grades, she might get another pony, or even a horse: Anne had been careful not to be specific about how or when this might happen.

'Poor you! Too bad of Jago Smith to blow the gaff prematurely.' Noel topped up her glass and added consolingly, 'Don't worry, her pony will have an excellent home. Such a nice family, and that boy isn't going to grow into a giant, no matter what his father thinks. He's a pleasure to deal with, unlike the other chap I'm embroiled with just now: that old crook Norrie MacAleese – what a nightmare! '

The name caught Anne's attention, just as he hoped. 'The trainer who was banned for doping? It was in the papers.'

'That's the guy. Nothing to do with racing, though. Just that the horse I sold him in the spring had a heart attack the first time he took it hunting, and now he's trying to sue me. Four months later – I ask you! He's out for blood, all right. Accuses me of bribing the vet to give him a clean bill of health, wants his money back or he'll have the law on me… threatens to sue, take me for every penny I've got etc etc. That's why I'm off to Yorkshire tonight, to see if I can calm him down.'

'What if you can't?' Anne asked, and he laughed.

'Then I'll tell him to go ahead and sue. Jonah says it would be better to settle out of court, but I'd like to see the old rogue get his comeuppance. Teach him to threaten me – now, what will you have next? The fish is good here. What about the *sole meunière*? Or lobster?'

It was so long since Anne had been taken out to dinner that the warmth and elegance of their surroundings plus the attentive service that The Duke's Arms lavished on a favourite customer soon restored her spirits, and she thought how lucky Helen was and what a fool Prue had been to ask this charming, amusing, civilised man for a divorce.

Coffee, crème de menthe, and petits fours were before them when Noel clapped a hand to his pocket and brought out a stiff blue envelope. 'Mustn't forget this, ' he said, handing it over with a laugh. 'I thought cash would be more useful. Now, have you had all you want? I hate to hurry away, but my train's due at 10.15 and if you really wouldn't mind giving me a lift to the station…'

'Of course not. Dear Noel, thank you so much! It's been a lovely evening. I really enjoyed it.'

'We must do it again,' he smiled. 'Now we'd better hustle, or I'll miss the train. Sure you don't mind driving me? I could get a taxi…'

'Lord, no! It's no bother. Will the doorman lend us a brolly? It's still pouring, by the looks of it.'

Huddling together under the doorman's big red and blue golfing umbrella they scuttled to where the Fiesta was parked, laughing as they splashed through puddles, and Noel handed it back to its owner as Anne zapped the lock.

'Hop in, you're getting soaked,' she said, diving into the driver's seat while Noel swung his long legs aboard and reached for the seat belt. Anne turned the key and there was a sharp click. Then the whole car erupted in a sheet of flame.

*****

Detective Chief Inspector Martin Robb emptied the reservoir of hen pellets into a bucket and turned the malfunctioning feed-hopper upside down on the kitchen table. With a pair of slanted tweezers he carefully extracted the single pellet that was wedged between the rings of the spring, obstructing the self-closing mechanism that denied access to the food to any rat bold enough to hoist itself on to the button. As he did so, the shutter snapped into the closed position, and he smiled.

'That'll foil the raiders,' he said.

'Brilliant, Dad. You are clever: I couldn't see why it wouldn't shut,' said his middle daughter, Sally, who worked as gamekeeper for a syndicate shoot. 'Must you really go back today? It's lovely having you here. I've got lots of other tricky little repair jobs I'm sure you could fix.'

'Very kind of you, darling, but I've got a stack of paperwork on my desk, and the sooner I get to grips with it the better.' Robb glanced at his watch. 'I wonder where Winter's got to? He said he'd be here at nine and it's twenty past already. Not like him to be late.'

'Perhaps some of your favourite people have glued themselves to...' Sally had begun when the landline rang.

Robb heard her say, 'Yes. Yes, he's here. Wait a sec...'

Paling visibly, she held out the receiver to her father. 'It's Jonah. Jonah Murray. He wants to talk to you. Says it's very bad news.'

# CHAPTER FOUR

THE FIRST STORM of grief had given way to exhausted acceptance before Helen began to think with any clarity about the circumstances of Noel's death, and the questions arising from them.

He had been heading north by train to deal with some trouble from the sale of another horse – that much she knew, because he had told her about it – but why hadn't he mentioned the dinner date with his former sister-in-law? Was it the first time he had taken Anne to an expensive restaurant? And, looming over all other questions like a great black cloud, was the one that mattered most to her: was he having an affair with Anne?

'I honestly don't know,' she said wretchedly to her father, as they sat over their second cups of coffee the morning after his arrival. Gus was crawling about under the table, hoping for a chance to stroke the tabby, who distrusted small humans and had removed himself to the shelf above the Belfast sink, well out of reach of sticky hands. 'He was automatically nice – chivalrous – friendly – call it what you like, to all women, so of course they loved him back. He…' she gulped and blew her nose – 'he said it was all an act and called it his stock-in-trade, but I don't think it was. More like part of his personality.

He could have seen that Anne was lonely and miserable and wanted to cheer her up, no more than that. Or they could have been having a rip-roaring affair. There's no way to tell.' She turned to her brother-in-law. 'What d'you think, Jonah? You knew him better than anyone.'

'I'd say that's a pretty fair summary of his character.' Jonah shifted uncomfortably and stretched out his injured leg. 'We need our clients to like and trust us – yes, I know what you think about horse dealers, Mr Robb – but there has to be a fair degree of trust before you risk your life by getting on an unknown horse, or putting your child up on one.'

'*Touché*,' murmured Robb.

Jonah went on, 'But sometimes my brother *did* lay it on a bit thick, and if things went wrong you got the kind of situation we're now facing with old MacAleese: threats and recriminations because the horse turned out less than perfect.'

'Or keeled over with a heart attack,' said Helen. 'I don't see how that could possibly be blamed on Noel, four months after the sale. More coffee, anyone?'

'Not by any reasonable person – no. But Norrie isn't reasonable, and you've both seen the messages he's been sending me. The police were very interested in those. Threats to sue. Threats of violence. I wouldn't put it past him to work himself into a lather and reckon it's worth setting a few thugs on to the bastard who wronged him.' He shook his head. 'Violence, yes. A punch-up in a car park: that's Norrie's style. But a bomb cold-bloodedly placed under a car... No. Not unless he's changed a lot since I knew him.'

'People do change,' said Robb. 'You said you tried to persuade your brother to meet him halfway? To settle out of court?'

'That's right. Paying him back half the horse's price was bound to cost less than going to Court, because you never know for certain which way the jury's going to jump, and it all takes so long anyway. OK, so that was my advice, but Noel wasn't having it. He said it would damage his reputation for straight dealing, whether he won or lost, and there was something personal in it, too. He and Norrie rubbed one another up the wrong way. Chalk and cheese.'

There was a silence. Then Robb said, 'And Anne Cutler? Do you think she was just collateral damage? Wrong person in the wrong place at the wrong time?'

Jonah thought about it for a moment, then nodded. 'I don't know *why* she was with him. The hotel staff were pretty clear that they had a decent dinner together and the waiter said that they were evidently very good friends but not, he thought, lovers. Waiters notice these things. He's a French boy who has only been there a few weeks, and he may have misread the situation completely, but in his opinion they were too polite to one another to be sharing a bed.'

Robb said, 'That's interesting – as far as it goes. There must have been diners at other tables who would have noticed them. I'll get a list and have a word with all of them.'

'You mean you'll stay and try to get to the bottom of it?' said Jonah.

'No better way of spending my last days of leave,' said Robb.

'Thanks, Dad.' A small corner of the black cloud that hung over Helen lifted a trifle, then clamped down again. 'Poor Candy! She's in a terrible state. She feels it's her fault for saying she wished Anne wasn't her mother – apparently they had a frightful row when Candy found that Little Orchid had been sold, and she said all sorts of things she regrets. I couldn't get her to stop crying and of course that set me off too. You'd better talk to her, Jonah. She'll listen to you.'

'Sure.' He eased his leg off the stool and stood supported by his single crutch. 'Her aunt Prue is on her way from London right now. She said she'd drop everything and come at once, and I guess she'll want to take her back with her.'

'And I guess she won't want to go,' said Helen. 'Fireball's all she's got now. I don't see her agreeing to leave him.'

'Ah, well. Let's see how things turn out,' said Jonah, and made for the door, halting on the threshold to say, 'Where is she now, by the way? Better warn her that her aunt Prue should arrive any moment.'

Halting under the shadow of the archway before entering the stable yard, Helen braced herself for the chorus of condolence she was bound to encounter. Most of the livery regulars had telephoned or emailed already, but the stable staff who had known Noel since he was a teenager were liable to be both hardest hit and most tongue-tied. It seemed surreal to see them all bustling about just as usual – horses tied up outside their boxes, buckets and haynets being filled – when for her everything had altered beyond recognition.

'D'you know where Candy is?' she asked Jeremy, who paused in his rhythmic strapping of Lucky Dip, Helen's reliable black mare. Noel had bought her at Hereford Sales despite a splint the size of a matchbox on her near fore, and for the past three seasons she had earned a steady hundred pounds every time she was hired, and never gone lame.

'Gone up the all-weather, I reckon,' muttered Jeremy. 'Poor kid! Ricky was takin' Democrat for a pipe-opener, and Johnny heard 'im askin' Candy if she'd care to come along. Nowt like a gallop to take yer mind off of things.' He raised his head to look her in the eye. 'We're all sorry for your loss, missus. Terrible – just terrible. Don't know what the world's comin' to.' He added in a lower tone, glancing round as if afraid of being overhead, 'That Jago was 'ere again an hour ago, 'anging around as usual. I sent 'im about 'is business. Can't seem to keep away from where 'e's not wanted.'

'Well done.' Helen moved away, adding, 'If you see Candy, say her aunt is coming to fetch her, and we're waiting for her up at the house.'

She made a quick round of the stables, checked the tack room, feed store and haybarn, and returned to find her father and Jonah greeting a willowy stranger with keen, piratical features and the same dark curly hair as Anne.

Prue, of course!

Briefly glimpsed at her own wedding two years ago, Anne's dashing elder sister who, when married to Noel, suffered from the green monster just as she had. First Wife and Second Wife, correction, First Widow and Second Widow greeted one another with wary handshakes and commiserations, while Jonah, like an ever-helpful sheepdog, watched for an opportunity to smooth things over.

'You'll stay the night, at least,' he said, as Robb extracted a smart leather grip from the boot of her racing green MG.

Prue gave him a long, considering look, then suddenly smiled – sun breaking through clouds. 'I didn't mean to. I thought I'd just dash down, pick up Candy, and scoot back through the rush-hour traffic, but now you suggest staying – well, it does sound enticing to see my old haunts again. Less disruptive to Candy, too, if we take things slowly.' She turned to Helen. 'Is that all right?'

'Of course.'

'Sure it doesn't make things awkward for you?'

'Why should it?'

'Well, you know. Both of us married to Noel…'

'I can't see that makes any difference,' said Helen doggedly. 'Something terrible has happened, and it's up to us to pick up the pieces. Candy's the one we've got to think of.'

'Of course. You're absolutely right. Where is she, by the way?'

'Must be still down at the stables. I'll go and fetch her while Jonah brings your stuff in.'

The kaleidoscope of stable activity had changed its pattern since she'd been at the house. Horses had returned to their boxes, water buckets filled and feeds were being distributed.

A muddy saddle had been dumped outside Fireball's box and from inside came the sound of sobbing. Helen opened the door.

'Candy?'

There was a sudden movement at the back of the stable and what had looked like a single figure broke into two.

'Just helping put on Fireball's rug,' called Jago Smith. 'I reckon he rolled in it and got mud into all the buckles.'

'Come out of there, both of you.' Helen voice crackled with anger. 'I'll see to Fireball. Candy, your aunt's up at the house, so hurry up there and don't keep her waiting. As for you, Jago…'

'All right, all right, I'm just off, keep your hair on,' he drawled with studied insolence, slouching past her and heading for his motorbike. 'Only trying to help.'

'Look here, Jago: if I want any help from you, I'll ask for it and until then…' But he was gone, straddling the bike with defiance in every line of him. A blast of exhaust which startled every animal in the yard and he was away over the cattle grid, leaving her fuming.

\*\*\*\*\*

'Tricky,' said Jonah, carefully removing bones from his fish before pushing it to the side of his plate with an air of defeat. 'Sorry, Hels. I know this is delicious but I'm just not hungry.'

'That's not like you,' said Prue, but Helen felt the same: a curious difficulty in swallowing even though she knew she ought to eat, and complete tastelessness of anything she did get down. Shock, sorrow – whatever it was that had killed her appetite – had to be lived through before normality could return.

Jonah patted his pockets and she said, 'Go ahead if you want to smoke. OK by you, Dad? Prue?'

'Thanks. It's only vaping.' Jonah lit up and inhaled with relief. 'Back to Candy,' he said. 'You can't just drag her off if she doesn't want to go. She's what? Thirteen? Fourteen? If she says she'll run away she probably will. I suggest you let her stay here with her pony for the time being. Hels and I will look after her and see off this blasted young man who seems fixated with her, and you can come down like a good aunt and see her whenever you want. How about that?'

'Perfect,' said Prue, too quickly for Helen to believe she had really thought it over. She herself could see a good many drawbacks to making herself responsible for the day-to-day care and well-being of a wilful teenager but, given Candy's orphaned state and absolute refusal to be parted from her pony, perhaps this was the only sensible solution for the moment, at least.

The smallest of nods from her father signalled that he thought the same.

'Fine by me,' she said.

'Then there's the question of money,' said Jonah. 'Specifically the eight thousand that Noel managed to get for Little Orchid. Was it cash or a cheque? If cash, was it blown up with the car? I'll have to ask Charles Moncrieffe.'

Robb looked away. 'I'm not listening.'

'Good. Now what else have we got to sort out? House, possessions, vehicles, school, the press, and God knows what else besides.' The lines on his face deepened, adding years to his age as he added grimly, 'Whoever thought he could murder my brother and get away with it has made a very big mistake.'

The ever-busy life of a livery stable didn't stop to give any of them time to catch up with all the extra work engendered by the tragedy. Horses still had to be fed, watered, mucked out, groomed, shod and exercised. Tack still had to be cleaned, forage supplies ordered and checked. Stable staff still had to be paid, and livery clients needed the same degree of attention and support they were used to.

It was a pleasant surprise to find that most of Suleiman's cuts and scrapes were mere surface wounds and healed without leaving marks. Only the stitched flap of skin on his chest needed daily attention, and even that promised to heal invisibly.

'McAndrew's a genius with a needle,' commented Jonah, making a close inspection. 'When his summer coat comes through you won't be able to see where it was.'

Half-done deals and appointments to view could be cancelled or postponed, but horse lorries still needed regular checks, machinery still broke down and, above and beyond all these daily tasks, the hunting season rolled relentlessly on and subscribers demanded their money's worth. Days before Christmas were precious; a hard January and February could lead to many cancelled hunting days when the ground was frozen and every gateway endangered horses' legs, or was so wet that even the most accommodating farmers would beg the Hunt to stay away. Fog was another hazard and so was deep snow.

'Really it's a miracle if we get three weeks' hunting in succession after Christmas,' said Jasmine Dymoke, checking her diary. 'All right for people who ski as well as hunt, of course, but it does seem a waste to leave your horse eating his head off while you head for the snowy slopes.'

'Where you break a leg so you can't do either,' grinned Ricky Owen.

Later, Helen would realise that being forced to put in eighteen-hour days to keep the yard running, and being obliged to interact with clients and customers as well as family had probably helped keep her mind from being overwhelmed by grief – most of the time, anyway. She was used to Noel's frequent absences, but until now there had always been the comforting knowledge that sooner or later he would return. A telephone call, 'Can you meet me off the 5.19?' or the scrunch of a car on gravel, the bang of the front door, all signals that he was back – kissing her, scooping up Gus and tossing him up to the ceiling, sniffing appreciatively at whatever was in the Everhot, bursting with life and vitality and stories of his travels.

Knowing none of that would ever happen again was painful beyond belief and sometimes she, like Candy, wanted simply to bury her face in a horse's warm mane and let the world go on without her.

Robb, meanwhile, was pursuing his own enquiries. The manager and maître d' of The Duke's Arms were helpful and sympathetic and had readily produced a list of all their customers dining that evening and shown Robb which tables they had occupied. 'Such a lovely gentleman, Mr Murray, and a great favourite with all our staff,' said Alexis, the portly olive-skinned manager. 'Who would have wanted to do a wicked thing like that? We do get some rough types here from time to time – they come for the boxing, mostly – but that evening it was only couples, two or three family celebrations, a hen party from Birmingham over against the back wall: noisy, yes, but harmless – let's see, who else?' He consulted his booking list.

'The lady from table 16,' put in Pierre-Ange, the young waiter. 'She texting while eating and sometimes she look round the tables like she wait for someone.'

'That's right,' said Alexis. 'I asked her if anyone would be joining her and she said no, he must have caught a later train, so she would go ahead and eat. Her table was nearest to Mr Murray's. If anyone overheard conversation it would have been her.'

'Thanks,' said Robb. 'I'd better have a word with her. Have you her contact details?'

\*\*\*\*\*

Ottilie Kennedy was busy in her garden – far too busy to want to talk to the police. She was a bottle-blonde with a small, discontented mouth and hair scraped back in a ballerina's high ponytail, and wore black leggings and an oversize cable-knit sweater in a bright shade of blue. Mutton dressed as lamb, thought Robb uncharitably as she swung round to face him with a frown that made clear she was not happy to be interrupted.

'Oh, not again! I've already talked interminably to the police and answered all their damn-fool questions,' she said brusquely when he explained his mission. 'I really don't want to go through it once more.'

'I can imagine,' he sympathised. 'The same questions over and over: it's enough to drive you mad. But it all helps to build up a picture – to fill in the jigsaw, if you like – and every small detail you remember may be important.'

She gave an exasperated sigh, then relented. 'OK. OK. But I warn you I can't remember very much. I wasn't paying attention to other diners because…' she smiled reluctantly – 'well, to be honest, I was in a foul temper. Everything had gone wrong that evening. A photographer I was meeting to discuss some publicity shots pulled out at the last minute, and then my husband missed his train, and his dinner, which was to have celebrated our wedding anniversary. So I was eating alone, and trying to fix up another date with this damned photographer, and frankly not paying much attention to my surroundings. There was a hen party behind me, shrieking their silly heads off, so it was pretty noisy.'

She wiped her gardening gloves across her forehead, leaving a smear of mud. 'Actually, I did just register a rather dishy number at the table to my right, because he was the sort women do notice: tall and well-dressed, quite hot and he had ordered champagne, which is another thing one tends to notice, but apart from that...'

'He was my son-in-law,' said Robb quietly, and she jumped as if she had touched an electric wire.

'Oh, I'm sorry! Really sorry. I didn't know...'

'How could you?'

'No. Of course not. The girl – well, woman – with him reminded me of someone, but I can't for the life of me think who it was.'

'She was his sister-in-law. That's to say, his former sister-in-law, before he married my daughter. Her name was Anne Cutler,' said Robb. 'She worked at the Confucius Centre over at Dorningdale.'

'Worked for those Chinese?' Her eyebrows rose. 'Can't say I'd envy her that job. The old ladies who used to run that school were great supporters of our annual flower show in aid of St Dunstan's. They hosted it on alternate years and always drew a big crowd, but the moment the Chinks took it over all that finished. Kaput. Letters telling us to keep our distance. I heard they did the same with the Hunt. Anne Cutler...' She frowned with the effort of memory.

'There used to be Cutlers living in this village. Rich. Big house, loads of servants, but there was a scandal of some sort. Anne could have been one of that family.'

She thought for a moment then shook her head. 'Doesn't ring a bell. My memory for faces isn't great, but there was something about her... Poor thing. Poor both of them. The police said they were killed instantly.'

'Yes. I'm trying to find out why.'

'Horrible.' She shuddered. 'They were really pushing the boat out, too. When I left the waiter was bringing all the kit for crêpes Suzette, and he was calling for Beaume de Venise.'

'So you didn't hear the bomb go off?'

'No, thank God. I must have been a couple of miles away by then, and the first I knew of it was hearing sirens.'

Robb glanced at his watch. It was half past eleven, and the pale winter sun was beginning to struggle through the veil of morning mist. Tall silvery grasses which fringed the path to the gate quivered in a breath of wind and brought to his nostrils a waft of scent that seemed out of season, warm – almost mimosa-like in its sweetness – and emerging from the shelter of glossy dark leaves, the creamy bells of hellebores broke covert with dramatic effect.

She was watching him, amused, as he tried to pinpoint where it was coming from. 'Tell me, what is that delicious smell?'

'Could be the mahonia, could be winter jasmine, could be one of the viburnums... I like to keep scented shrubs for the months when there's not much colour and, of course, our visitors from St Dunstan's love it.'

She had dropped her hostility and spoke with the enthusiasm of a true gardener. 'Come over to the summerhouse for a minute. You get all kinds of different scents there.' She led the way to an octagonal wooden structure in the middle of a rose garden. Just a few blooms clung to the tall stalks, ('Can't bear to hack them down yet,') but the moment he sat down on the curved slats of a chair, he began to catch wafts of other scents from trees and shrubs planted in a protective shelterbelt round the rose beds.

'Wonderful,' he exclaimed, inhaling deeply. 'In winter one forgets how much one relies on a sense of smell until you catch something like this.'

Ottilie looked pleased. 'I'm glad you're enjoying it. We try to fill the beds with fragrant plants all year round – actually a lot of these old roses came from Brenda and Jane Rigby's garden. The Chinese threw them out and the groundsman saved them for us. They transplanted very well, considering how ancient they must be. Roses are much more resilient than one imagines.'

'Well, nice as it is here, I must drag myself away.' Robb got up, dusting the seat of his trousers. 'I've taken up quite enough of your time.'

'Wait one,' she said. 'I've remembered something I heard of that poor couple's conversation. He – your son-in-law...'

'Noel.'

'Right: well, Noel was telling Anne about how difficult his clients could be when it came to buying horses. Apparently he was getting some grief from a character called MacAleese: I remember because it's an odd name and I know I've seen it before. Norrie MacAleese.'

Breakthough, thought Robb. Always at the last minute. 'That's right,' he said. 'Banned for doping. There was a court case and he was lucky not to be gaoled. Can you remember what Noel said?'

'Not exactly, but he implied they'd had rows in the past. Then something like, 'He's out for blood this time,' which I remembered because it sounded so OTT.'

'Thank you, that's very helpful,' said Robb. 'If anything else occurs to you, do get in touch with me. I'm staying with my daughter, but here's my mobile number.'

Confirmation, he thought, driving back to Barleycourt, but of the flimsiest kind. Third-hand conversation overheard in a noisy restaurant was not going to impress any jury, and it did nothing to answer the question of why Anne had been there. Dressed to the nines, according to the young waiter, she had come out to meet Noel on a wet, windy winter night; she had offered him a lift to the station to catch the train north; the bomb had been under her car. Was it possible that it had been meant for her rather than Noel?

What did he know about Anne Cutler? A single mother with a half-Chinese daughter, living in a rented cottage and working in some unspecified role for the Confucius Centre. Why had she chosen to ally herself with a shadowy and locally unpopular organisation? What was her connection to China?

Helen's grief was too raw, her loss too recent, and her fear that Anne had been Noel's mistress too overwhelming for her to discuss these questions easily. Jonah might have some answers, he thought; better still would be the opinion of Noel's former wife, the dashing and outspoken Prudence, who would probably appreciate a break from the grim task of sorting and disposing of her sister's clothes while her niece was at school.

No time like the present, he thought, tapping the Centre's postcode into his satnav; twenty minutes later he was staring at a distinctly unwelcoming notice on high wrought-iron gates: *Visitors by appointment only* and wondering if they would open automatically. Winking red CCTV eyes stared back at him. After waiting a moment, he put his hand on the horn and eventually a burly, shaven-headed Chinese man in a dark-blue tunic sauntered out of the kiosk on the left-hand side.

'Visitor not allowed,' he said flatly.

Robb considered pulling rank, but before he could do more than burrow under his anorak for ID, a muddy Kawasaki drew up beside the driver's window.

'You looking for Anne Cutler's cottage?' said Jago Smith, helmetless and wearing only a sweatshirt despite the cold. He leaned in through the window, emitting a pungent aroma of hash. 'She don't live inside the gates – that's to say, she didn't. Her sister's there now, packing up her things. Follow me and I'll show you.'

He roared off, spraying mud and gravel. Half a mile round the perimeter wall and down a double-tracked farm lane leading into the woods, he pulled up outside an isolated brick cottage set back on a semi-circle of rough lawn and surrounded by a ragged hedge. The front door was open, the steps were piled high with suitcases and boxes, and parked outside, looking thoroughly out of place, was Prue's smart little sports car.

What a dump! thought Robb, and then, what a perfect hideaway. Trees and overgrown shrubs might once have made an attractive garden, but they had not been pruned for years, and the ivy smothering the walls was reaching tentative fingers towards every window on the ground floor.

He waved his thanks to Jago, who pointed at the house, sketched a salute and zoomed on down the track, which evidently led to a road. A moment later Prue appeared in the doorway with yet another load of boxes. She greeted him with a cry of delight.

'Glory be! The Seventh Cavalry – just when it's most needed!' she exclaimed. 'Can you give me a hand? Some of this stuff is too heavy for me to shift on my own, and that useless boy says he's far too busy to help. I want to get everything packed and stacked before Candy gets back on the school bus, then the removals van can collect it in the morning.'

'We'll do it together,' said Robb, getting out of the car.

For such a small house, it contained an astonishing amount of possessions. Prue tackled the clothes, sorting them into heaps for Oxfam, recycling, and rubbish with efficiency and dispatch, while Robb busied himself stripping the kitchen of equipment and emptying the cupboards into innumerable crates.

'It was let furnished, thank God,' said Prue, 'so we needn't worry about beds and stuff, and I know which of the sheets and towels belonged to my sister.'

They worked mostly in silence, carrying the heavy stuff between them, and when at last everything was packed and it was barely possible to move in the little hallway, they stood back and admired the wall of crates neatly squared up for the removal men.

'Thanks, Martin, I'd never have managed it without you.' Stripping off rubber gloves, Prue heaved a sigh of relief and ran her fingers through her hair. 'I was on the point of throwing in the towel when you turned up like an answer to prayer.'

Robb nodded. 'How about a drink? And a bite? I think we've earned it.'

She followed him in her car to a promising-looking pub he had spotted on the outskirts of Dorningdale. 'Oh, this is nice,' she said, walking into the bar and gazing around before settling at a table against the wall while Robb ordered.

She said, 'I'm sure this pub was one of Dad's favourites in the happy old days before our troubles began.'

'Will you tell me about that?' Seeing her hesitate, he added, 'I'd like to understand how your sister came to be living in such an isolated cottage...'

'And working for such a strange outfit?' She stared into her G&T. 'To be honest, I never understood it either. Anne could be pretty secretive. For instance, she never told me who was – or is – Candy's father, though he was obviously someone she met in Hong Kong when she worked out there for our uncle. She didn't exactly warn me off questions; more that there were certain areas in Anne's life where one just didn't go.'

'You mean she was ashamed of them? For instance of being an unmarried mother?'

She laughed. 'Lord, no! That's no big deal nowadays. No, I think she liked having secrets: look how she kept schtum about selling Candy's pony until she was absolutely forced to admit it. On the other hand she was perfectly open about needing money. I understood that, all right, and helped her when I could, which wasn't a lot but may have helped. She was always dreaming up crazy schemes of how to make a fortune – and there again I gave a hand when I could. Quite recently, in fact...' She stopped abruptly, as if afraid of saying too much.

Or remembering who she was talking too, thought Robb. Interesting. He wondered if one of those crazy schemes had involved breaking the law.

He said, 'Would you say you were pretty close as children?'

'Oh, yes.' Her sudden blush faded: she was back in her comfort zone. 'Peas in a pod. United in opposition to Mummy, who liked to keep us busy – have you done this, cleaned that, exercised your ponies; can't leave it all to the grooms, you know – and adoration of Dad, who was exactly the opposite, and would have liked us to do nothing but sit on a cushion and sew a fine seam and eat chocolates all day long. We both thought that money grew on trees, and it was a fearful shock to find that everything – *everything* – we believed was ours actually belonged to the bank.' She added almost in a whisper, 'I think that was the moment when I grew up; but Anne, who was a three years younger, never did.'

She was silent, staring back down the years. Robb said, 'How old were you then?'

'Oh...fourteen or fifteen. Old enough to know what bankrupt meant. Mum told me I'd better buck up my ideas because I was going to have to earn a living: I think she had seen this coming a long way off. So I bucked them up and got a degree in biology, and that was useful when my marriage to Noel came unstuck.' She looked curiously at him. 'Tell me, what did you really think of Noel? Did you like him? Were you pleased that your daughter wanted to marry him?'

Boot on other foot time, thought Robb. Now she is planning to grill me. Aloud he said, 'It was difficult not to like him, but if you're asking did I trust him, I'm afraid the answer is no. Horse dealers have a bad reputation and frankly Noel seemed a bit too good to be true. Just a touch too much of the golden boy about him, and so many of them turn out to have feet of clay. Too darned attractive, in other words. That sounds so petty, but I couldn't see him sticking to one woman when every girl he met was batting her eyelashes at him. You may laugh – but no, I wasn't at all pleased that Helen wanted to marry him and I did my level best to dissuade her. It won't surprise you to hear that nothing I said had the least effect.'

'I'm not laughing,' said Prue soberly, 'because it was the same with my Mum and for much the same reasons. But you were both wrong, you know. He really *was* a nice guy, and quite as straightforward as his brother; the difference being that while most people instinctively trust Jonah to tell them the worst about a horse, they tended to think Noel was concealing something.' She smiled suddenly, '*Of course* no animal is perfect! If it was, why would you sell it? The question is whether or not it is worth the price you're asking? Worth it to *you*?'

Robb digested this. 'Are you telling me that Noel would knowingly sell a bad horse if he could get away with it?'

Prue shook her head vigorously. 'That's exactly what I'm *not* saying. *He* would know to a penny how much that animal was worth, how much trouble it was likely to give the buyer, both physically and psychologically – or how much the buyer might profit from it…'

Robb was shaking his head. 'Stop. I'm afraid you've lost me. Go back to Noel. Why did you two split up? It sounds to me as if you were well suited.'

'That's what I thought too. What I hoped, but – there's always a but, isn't there? – the truth is I couldn't stand the way women ran after him, and he encouraged them to. Said there was safety in numbers and it was good for business. Well, I daresay it was, but it was horrible for me.'

'I can well imagine,' said Robb, who had picked up the tail end of this complaint from Helen, too. 'Was your sister one of the women who ran after Noel?'

'Anne? No, that was when she was working abroad. By the time she and Candy came back my marriage was a thing of the past. Actually I was surprised that she chose to settle here, considering how nasty people had been to Mum and her when Dad was sent down.'

'Where is your mother now?'

'In what's called sheltered accommodation in Yorkshire, though it's more like a comfortable cage. I go to see her when I can, but I'm not sure that she recognises me.' Her eyes filled with tears and she brushed them away impatiently. 'Mum's OK as far as it goes, though that's not very far.'

Time for another drink, thought Robb, looking at her empty glass, but Prue turned down the suggestion in favour of food. Any food. The bar was steadily filling with noise and chatter, but their corner settle still felt private enough until there was a flutter of trailing scarves and gold chains, a waft of Je Reviens, and a hand with vivid turquoise nails came over the back to descend on Prue's shoulder.

'Darling, I'm sorry! I'm so, so sorry! We're all devastated,' said flamboyantly dressed Jasmine Dymoke, swathed in a purple silk caftan and shocking pink tights. 'We were on our way out to lunch when Ricky spotted your MG in the car park and we knew you must be in here.' She followed up her words with a hug, and in a moment it seemed they were surrounded by horsy friends bombarding Prue with condolences and sympathy. The newcomers settled on the other side of the table, pulling up chairs, chattering nonstop while Prue made introductions as smoothly as a croupier deals cards.

'Jasmine Dymoke; Ricky Owen; Isabel Garraway; Harvey... Dora... Marjorie... I'd like you to meet Martin Robb, Helen's father...'

He nodded, said little, listened to them talk. Several, it seemed, kept horses at Barleycourt. All were clearly shocked at the way violent death had invaded their peaceful lives; no one had a bad word to say about either of the victims or a good one about Norrie MacAleese.

'He's mixed up in a lot of dirty business,' said Ricky darkly. 'My cousin's Clerk of the Course at Beverley and he says whenever there's trouble on race days you can be sure Norrie or his mates will be at the bottom of it.'

Noel, however, came in for a lot of praise; evidently he had been a favourite with men as well as women. Ricky again: 'I'd never have even considered buying Democrat until he talked me into it. When I saw the poor fellow on that bare windy field in February, looking like a huge toast rack covered in mud and cat hairs, I thought all he was fit for was the knacker, but Noel said if I didn't buy him, he would, and charge me double for him in three months' time, so I took the plunge...'

'Like me with Betsinda,' trilled Jasmine. 'I mean, I fell head over heels in love with her at first sight, but the price they were asking was *ridiculous*. I couldn't begin to pay that. Then Noel pointed out lots of small *défauts* I hadn't noticed and, long story short, he got them to drop two thousand five hundred off the asking price...'

Well-dressed, articulate professionals in mid-career, with different backgrounds, different skills, but united in their obsession with horses, talking endlessly about them in their own peculiar language, fascinating to themselves but deeply boring to non-speakers; plotting, dealing, and no doubt dreaming about horses, and certainly spending an absurdly high proportion of their taxed income on their care and well-being. Robb couldn't understand it, but he recognised the strength of an obsession when he met it. He also knew how thin was the line between a fit, sound, valuable horse and one which a misstep, a fall, an infection could render lame and virtually worthless. All those dreams, all that care and money, could vanish in the blink of an eye.

Not a risk I would willingly undertake, he thought, making his excuses and taking his leave. He had work to do.

*****

Ottilie was at home but in a rush to go out when he rang her. Robb wondered if her whole life was one long rush to catch up with all the people she had promised to help. 'Who? Martin Robb?' she said edgily then in a more friendly tone, 'Ah, yes, the scent-loving cop. I'm so sorry to disappoint you, but I have thought and thought without remembering anything else, and now I'm late for...'

'This won't take a minute. When we talked about those roses you saved from the bonfire at Dene Manor, I think you said the old ladies sent you a Christmas card.'

'That's right.'

'Was there an address on it, by any chance?'

'Oh yes, I know their address. After selling Dene Manor they moved to London: it's Loxbury House, Loxbury Crescent, Barnum Road, N something. I can never remember postcodes.

North London, anyway. I'll give them a buzz right away if you like. Now I really must fly. Give the old pets my love, won't you?'

She rang off, and Robb felt the satisfaction of a punter whose long shot has come off. Like Jonah, he didn't believe in leopards changing their spots, or racecourse thugs their methods of exacting revenge.

*****

A neo-Georgian development in rosy brick, with neat car ports, cream paintwork and identical deep-blue front doors, Loxbury Crescent fully lived up to the house agents' description of 'manicured'. Each hedge might have been trimmed with a spirit level, so smooth and even were the tops; the little oblongs of lawn were uniformly flat and green, edged with narrow flowerbeds which were no doubt colourful in summer but in their stripped-back winter tidiness had a depressing effect: nature tamed into subservience, its spirit entirely crushed by strimmers, clippers, mowers, leaf blowers and all the tools of modern garden care.

In this sterile setting, just one house stood out: a three-storey Victorian mansion whose peeling paint and large dirty windows set it apart from the rest of the crescent. The original big house, Robb thought, whose owners must have sold off a paddock or two to developers.

Beyond it, Barnum Road was a bustling thoroughfare with a bus stop, a children's playground, and even a corner shop, but once he swung the car into Loxbury Crescent he found it impossible to park without obstructing someone's entrance. After making a couple of three-point turns in search of a berth, he parked boldly across the gateway of the big Victorian mansion.

Here nature had been allowed to run wild. The meandering garden path was puddled with recent rain, and over it a double line of weeping birches swept their fragile branches like a guard of honour presenting arms. Thickets of head-high *Rugosa* roses pressed in on the path, with an underlying carpet of entwined and entangled ground cover… What had once been a lawn was now more like a tussocky field; even in daylight rabbits were nibbling at the edges and the die-straight nocturnal routes of badgers were plain to see.

'Our visitor, Brenda!' shrilled a voice from an upstairs window as he rang the doorbell, 'Wait a minute, please. I'm on my way,' but it was nearer five minutes before the rattle of a lock heralded the appearance of a plump old lady like a well-stuffed cushion, with bubble-cut white hair and a smile that radiated beneficence. Her brown eyes were enmeshed in wrinkles and sparkled with goodwill. Over a black silk dress she wore a pillar-box red quilted gilet, and her neat little feet were encased in shiny black slip-ons.

Behind her drifted a very different figure, thin, vague and wispy, whose smile – though welcoming – raised doubt that she knew where she was or whom it was directed at. Jane Rigby was dressed in a curious assortment of outdoor and indoor garments, a hand-knitted scarf and beret over what looked like pyjamas, and solid brown mid-calf hiking boots.

'Mr Robb? Come in, come in! Dear Ottilie told us she hoped you would call today. This is my sister, Jane.'

Good for Ottilie, thought Robb, following her down a black-and-white tiled passage and into a chintzy sitting room. This was more than he had expected. 'She asked me to give you her love and tell you the old roses are flourishing. In fact, she thinks the move has given them a new lease of life.'

Miss Brenda's smile faded. 'I wish you could say the same of us! There's nothing we regret more than selling Dene to those terrible people, but the truth is, we were misled.'

'It was all going to be so different,' confirmed her sister in a soft, plaintive murmur.

Sitting at the scrubbed wooden table, Miss Brenda outlined the circumstances in which the Chinese had acquired Dene Manor, while Miss Jane silently laid plate after plate of small delicious cakes in front of Robb as if he had been a ravenous schoolboy.

'If Ottilie has asked us to come back once, she has asked a dozen times,' said Miss Brenda, 'but we can't face seeing the changes in dear Dene. We'd rather remember it how it was when we lived there with all the children shouting and laughing, and running about the grounds.'

'It was a place full of joy,' said Miss Jane, blinking rapidly and blowing her nose. 'We gave our pupils everything they wanted to make them happy. But after the Inspector's report said cruel things about a lack of discipline and rated us unsatisfactory, so many parents took their children away that we knew we couldn't go on.'

'So unfair,' murmured Robb. 'Your finances must have been on a knife's edge, too.'

'I knew you would understand.' Miss Brenda beamed at him. 'So we tried to find a buyer who would continue to run a school there and that's what the Chinese promised to do. We were so happy to think of dear little Chinese children learning their times tables in the classrooms, and playing their tiny violins…'

'But that's not what happened?'

Miss Brenda's face darkened. 'They lied to us. All they wanted was to create an institute where they could brainwash students into promoting the Chinese Communist Party. No children, no cultural events: just politics, politics all the way. We hear from old friends like Ottilie that they've changed the place completely – it's more like a fortress than a school now. They ripped out all our flowerbeds and most of the shrubs, but dear Jago calls on us from time to time and brings bulbs from the woodland garden which he plants here to remind us of our lovely Dene! It's enough to make you weep.'

Afraid that she might suit the action to the word, Robb hurriedly changed the subject. 'You've chosen a beautiful spot here. It's hard to believe that we're inside the M25. So green and peaceful.'

'Except when our neighbours start on their gardens at weekends!' said Miss Jane with unexpected tartness. 'Lovely people, all of them, but they are such townies. They like everything to be neat and tidy, and we get plenty of complaints about our little wildlife haven. They think the jungle will take over their gardens if they don't keep chopping and mowing and cutting off every new shoot that dares to show its face.'

'I must say I prefer a sweet disorder in the dress of any garden,' said Robb and she gave a crow of pleasure.

'That's what I tell our neighbours. Do try an eclair, Mr Robb, or perhaps you'd like a slice of gingerbread?'

Useless to protest that he'd put on weight. When he left after another half hour of gentle, unrelenting pressure to eat, Robb groaned faintly as he eased his belt a hole. I need exercise, he thought.

A few hundred yards beyond Loxbury Crescent, a fingerpost pointed the way to Wanderedge Common, and abandoning his car in a lay-by beside a green bin with dire warnings to dog-owners, Robb followed a couple of Barbour-clad, waxed-cotton-hatted thirty-something women setting a good pace uphill towards the green expanse of a considerable common. Walking decorously on leads beside them was an assortment of terriers and spaniels. Aha, locals, he thought, increasing his stride.

'Lovely morning,' he said as he overtook them.

'Better than yesterday,' they agreed, giving him the rapid once-over usually accorded by dog-walkers to the dog-free, and continuing to chat.

Just when he was wondering what it would take to start a conversation, they all turned their heads as a lugubrious bellow of 'Taar-quin!' sounded behind them.

The women rolled their eyes. 'Poor Edwin. Not again,' said Terrier-Walker. Spaniel-Walker nodded.

'Hasn't a clue. That dog runs rings round him.'

'But not *round* him, exactly. Just listen to those birds! Goes through them like a knife through butter. Watch out, he's coming this way.'

'Taar-quin! Here, boy! Here!' pleaded the voice, and a moment later a portly bald man with a scarlet face appeared on the track below, a lead swinging uselessly from his hand. He shouted, 'I've lost my dog. Have you seen him?' and that instant a large black labrador emerged from the dead bracken and bounded towards them panting and grinning.

Both women swiftly drew their dogs aside and shielded them with their legs. 'Don't want them catching fox mange,' said one, waving her stick at Tarquin, who was keen to fraternise. 'Go home, you brute. Grr!'

With a swift pounce, Robb seized Tarquin by the scruff and held him long enough to unbuckle his belt with the other hand and slip it round the dog's neck.

'Well done!' said the women in unison. 'That dog's a menace.'

'Well done!' said Edwin, arriving a few minutes later. He looked on the verge of apoplexy. 'Thank you. I thought he was gone for good. Jumped out past me the moment I opened the boot. I never had a chance to put him on the lead. I'm most grateful to you, sir.'

'Don't mention it,' said Robb, embarrassed. He said to change the subject, 'I don't know this area. It's quite a surprise to find such a big common in the midst of so much housing.'

'And long may it stay that way,' said Spaniel-Walker heartily. 'We're pretty quick on the draw when developers come sniffing round Wanderedge, and largely thanks to Edwin here we've managed to keep them at bay.'

'So far,' put in Terrier-Walker.

'It's an ongoing struggle,' confirmed Edwin, who had recovered his breath. 'We can't let down our guard for a moment.' He put on his cap and substituted Tarquin's lead for Robb's belt. 'Well, I'll be on my way and leave you good ladies to enjoy your walk. Thank you again, sir. Come on, Tarkie.'

They watched him walk away with the reluctant labrador dragging behind. 'He's a KC,' said Terrier-Walker. 'Top flight. He does a lot of planning work, appeals, that sort of thing. We're lucky to have him as Chair of Wanderedge Conservation Group. But he's definitely not a dog man.'

Both women laughed, and Robb said, 'Some people just aren't.'

The track grew steeper. For a few minutes they walked in silence, then Terrier-Walker said, 'That was quick of you to grab Tarquin. He's always escaping on to the Common, where he picks up fox mange and spreads it all over the place. Foxes are quite a problem here, largely thanks to those two old girls at the end of the road. Schoolmarms. Their garden is the most frightful mess. They never cut back the vegetation and actively *encourage* foxes to breed under their summerhouse. I was round there once, collecting for St Dunstan's – they're great supporters – and they showed me a whole litter of cubs peeking out from under the decking. I must say, they were sweet, but when they grow up they're far too bold and do a lot of damage.'

'What kind of damage?'

'Oh, you hear horrible stories! Cats mauled. Pet rabbits killed – they dig under the wire of runs – and nobody dares keep hens any longer. They gnaw the rubber off the aerials of cars and slide down the windscreens making a frightful mess, paw prints everywhere, and you often see them going through the bins in broad daylight. A woman who lives at the end of the crescent actually found a vixen upstairs in the nursery where her toddler was asleep.'

'Can't the pest officer get rid of them?' asked Robb.

She pulled a face. 'He's perfectly useless, poor man. He's not allowed to put out poison, and there's no way he could shoot them without a fearful outcry from – ahem – 'animal-lovers.' He's scared of being trolled on social media.'

'The main trouble is that they're not afraid of humans,' said her friend. 'I was at a dinner party the other evening where I heard people talking about a chap who's apparently a genius at getting rid of foxes. All very hush-hush and they wouldn't tell me his name.'

'How does he do it?' asked Robb, but she shook her head slowly and put a finger to her lips.

'They just say he's magic. One call to him, and your fox problem disappears. Of course he costs an arm and a leg.'

I bet I know who that is, thought Robb.

*****

Driving back to Barleycourt on the M4, he wondered what to do about Jago Smith's private hustle. Unethical, clearly, but was it actually illegal to move animals – well, pests – from a place where they were a day-to-day aggravation to one in which they would more naturally occur? If pest officers were powerless to remove them from cities, was it in order for Jago and his mates to take on the job? According to the dog-walkers, he must be making money at both ends of the operation: first from the house-proud owners of property cleared of their unwelcome guests, and secondly from buyers of fox skins. It was not difficult to guess who that would be.

A country life for urban foxes, where prey abounded in the form of rabbits and pheasants, rodents and worms, sounded ideal until you came up against the darker question: could an adult fox, which had lived all its life on thrown-out takeaways and human rubbish, learn how to hunt for its own food? If not, it would soon starve, and whoever was responsible for translocating it would be liable to a charge of causing unnecessary suffering to an animal.

As a boy, prowling the hedgerows of his uncle's farm with a 20-bore in the hope of picking up a brace of rabbits, Robb had seen enough of wildlife to know how wary and quick to disappear any prey species becomes. Even hunting cats with their formidable reserves of patience and agility often missed their mark: how many careful stalks were needed to secure a meal? How many times did they return empty-bellied?

He thought it unlikely that any fox whelped under the Misses Rigby's summer house and given the remains of their Sunday joint since cubhood could adapt to a regime of self-sufficiency in the Chiltern beechwoods where every man's hand was against it. Farmers defending their hen houses and armed gamekeepers would soon make an end of it, not to mention packs of foxhounds who were not allowed to hunt foxes but might not have quite understood the prohibition.

A grey area, he concluded, but one that was certainly win-win for Jago Smith. It would be interesting to hear Jonah's thoughts on the matter.

*****

Since she had found herself, however unwillingly, *in loco parentis* to Candy Cutler, Helen had become increasingly anxious about her charge. On several occasions she found her sobbing quietly in her pony's stable, and although most of her livery clients did their best to cheer her up, they all had jobs and families so their time at Barleycourt was limited. After all, that was why they paid sky-high fees to have their horses royally looked after, and Helen was determined they should get their money's worth.

The stable staff were sympathetic, but they, too, were always busy. She herself, as their boss, found it hard not to snap at them to get on with their work when she saw Seamus allowing Candy to drive his mini-tractor and scattering bedding about the yard, or Jem letting her mix feeds in the wrong proportions. Stable management with a yard full of horses was a demanding business; having a grief-stricken teenager mooning about just made it that much more difficult.

Where Candy was undoubtedly a blessing, however, was in her enthusiasm for playing with Gus. She never seemed to tire of cuddling him, dressing and bathing him, and making him laugh with silly games – whereas I, thought Helen guiltily, quickly get bored with looking after my own child and yearn for the moment I can put him to bed. A shameful admission, but it's no use pretending I'm much of a mother. I *do* love him, but I can't help finding him a crashing bore. Perhaps it will be different when he's older. At the moment even Dad – even Jonah – are better at amusing him than I am.

It didn't help that he reminded her piercingly of Noel: same shape, same colour blue eyes; same way of throwing his head back when he laughed, same fair hair growing to a point in the nape of his neck. Every time she looked at him she remembered what she had lost and how short had been their time together. It was deeply unfair to blame the little boy for resembling his father, but nothing in life is fair and at some subconscious level she did wish he could have taken his looks from her side of the family.

After some thought, she had given Candy a room next to the nursery where Gus slept, and retained the intercom connecting both these rooms to the main house so that Jonah could hear what was going on when she was down at the stables. Her father had a bigger room up a half-flight of steps, overlooking the park.

On the other side of the landing was a long low room piled high with the boxes of Anne's possessions salvaged from her cottage, plus a bed and bathroom for Prue to use on her frequent visits.

'Don't beat yourself up about it,' advised Prue briskly when Helen voiced her worries about Candy. 'The poor kid's lost her mother; she's bound to grieve and blame herself for that row they had just before Anne was killed. That was the most wretched luck – that it should have happened the very day they'd had a major set-to but, you know, it wasn't uncommon. They were always shouting at one another. Anne had a low flashpoint and Candy's no slouch when it comes to slanging matches.'

Helen was only partially reassured. Another worry was the very long rides Candy had taken to having in the woods. One of the chief selling points for Barleycourt's location as a livery stable was the way it was surrounded by the extensive beechwoods which stretch almost unbroken for many miles in north Oxfordshire, together with their tracks – bridleways, tractor routes and forestry tracks – providing riders with an abundance of stress-free hacking.

Here and there the woods were intersected by minor roads, but generally speaking there was very little traffic, no unwelcoming notices, and no worries that they might suddenly come on an enraged landowner and be ordered to leave.

'Just shut any gate you open, and tell me or Jonah if any of the paths are blocked,' Helen would say when briefing a new client. 'We often get trees down after a strong wind, and it's useful to know where needs clearing. Apart from that, you can pretty much ride where you please, but do take a mobile with you.'

Candy was scrupulous about carrying her smartphone wherever she went, and Helen had no doubt that she could call her at any time, but the length of time she spent hacking alone in the woods had become a nagging worry.

'Wouldn't it be more fun to go with someone else?' she suggested as Candy mounted Fireball one sunny morning.

'Not really, thanks.'

Well, that's clear enough, thought Helen, but she gave it another try. 'Ricky's always looking for someone to keep that crazy Democrat calm.'

Candy's face became inscrutable; very Chinese, thought Helen. She said, 'What would we talk about? Ricky and I aren't interested in the same things. Besides, I like being alone with my thoughts.'

That's what worries me, Helen thought, imagining depression, self-harm and other horrors on top of more mundane troubles like Fireball going lame or casting a shoe, Candy losing her way in the woods or being confronted by a weirdo.

'Should I put some kind of tracker on her?' she asked her father, but he shook his head decisively.

'I wouldn't dream of it. Give the poor kid some space – after all she's suffered a major loss and still has to get over that. You don't want to make her feel she's living in a police state.'

So Helen did nothing, but gradually the conviction grew on her that Candy was meeting someone in the woods, and the most likely candidate was Jago Smith. Since her ultimatum, he had not been hanging about the stable yard, but that meant nothing. Should she challenge the girl directly, or would that simply compound the problem?

She would not have been reassured had she known how carefully Candy was covering her tracks by setting off in a different direction every day, and giving a false report of where she and the pony had been, acting on strict instructions from the thin-faced Hong Kong activist in a broad-brimmed fedora known to her as Uncle William.

He was waiting, as promised, under the biggest of the ash trees that formed a little grove a hundred yards off the single-track road to The Crooked Scythe, a country pub that had not moved with the times and was almost deserted on weekdays.

She dismounted and bowed to him as Anne had taught her.

'Tie up your horse,' he said by way of greeting, 'and see what I have brought for you today. But first I wish to know how are your grades at school, and are you yet top of your class? Are you in the team for netball?'

It didn't bother her that he never showed overt affection, or his ignorance of school and its hierarchy. She thanked him for the small square box with its promising sweet smell, and answered his quick, staccato questions, glad to have someone from her old life taking an interest in her doings, reminding her of her mother. Everyone else did their best not to talk about Anne. Even Aunt Prue wouldn't tell her why or by whom a bomb had been attached to her mother's car, but Uncle William said without hesitation that the police would find out and whoever had done it would be punished.

'You don't know that. They might never find them,' she said gloomily and was immediately rebuked.

'Where are your manners, Candy? Did your mother not teach you it is not polite in children to contradict their elders?'

She hung her head. 'I am sorry.'

'Then listen when I speak and do not question what I say. I have enemies and they have many eyes, so I must always keep moving, and you must never, never speak of me to anyone. Do you understand? Have I your promise?'

'Yes.'

'You are a good child,' he said to her surprise, because praise from him was rare. 'One day when you are older I will tell you the reason for this secrecy, but until then you must be obedient.'

'I am so tired of being obedient,' she said dolefully, and saw the deep grooves in his cheeks smooth out as he smiled.

'Soon I will meet you again, and until then work hard in your school and remember what your mother taught you.'

She was itching to interrupt again and ask why he had to be constantly on the move, but he pre-empted the question. 'My enemies accuse me of sedition – you know what that means?'

'No, but...'

'Look it up.'

His head turned sharply as a vintage motorbike with a red sidecar appeared *pop-pop-popping* along the road, heading towards the pub. Fireball had a deep suspicion of machines that made popping noises. He snorted, rolled his eyes and pulled back against his tether. Candy stepped forward to calm him and, when she looked round again, Uncle William had vanished.

Slowly, with many glances over her shoulder in case he suddenly reappeared, she untied the lead-rope from its branch and remounted. Comforted by his assurance of another meeting soon, she rode back to the stables.

# CHAPTER FIVE

'BORROW YOUR CAR, sis?'

Fern did not respond at once. Things lent to Jago had a habit of coming back with bits missing, and she relied on her sturdy little green van to get her mobile hairdressing equipment to clients who lived out in the sticks, often in inaccessible places.

'Why mine? Why not take Reuben's old heap of scrap metal as per usual?'

'Off the road,' said Jago, sauntering into the kitchen and looking round. 'Argument with a bollard on Saturday night, and the body shop say it can't be driven without extensive repairs. Where's Corky, then?'

'Search me,' she said indifferently. 'Haven't seen him for days. Look, Jago, if I lend you my van, you better bring it back with a full tank. And I don't want it covered in mud, either.'

She surveyed him critically: a big lad, handsome if you liked the dark-eyed, wolfish type – she preferred something less bristly – but he was doing well for himself, no doubt about that. By all accounts he had his bosses at the Centre eating out of his hand. His hair was cut straight across his forehead like a footballer and long enough at the back to curl over his collar.

'You could do with a trim,' she told him. 'Looks like you been dragged through a hedge backwards. Who gave you that cut?'

He followed her into her bedroom to sit at her dressing table without protest, and watched in the mirror while she combed and snipped, sorting out the layers to her liking.

'So where are you off to in my van?' she asked, putting a slight stress on the car's ownership.

'London. Got to fetch a load of stuff for the Centre. They're short-handed since the Cutler woman was killed, and they've got bigwigs coming over for this anniversary. Twenty-five years since the handover of Hong Kong, innit?'

Fern wasn't interested in politics. She said, 'Police found out yet who done it? And what about that kid used to ride pillion on your bike? What's happened to her? '

'Her aunt's let them take her in at Barleycourt, so's she can stay with her pony till school finishes. Exams or summat,' said Jago vaguely.

'Poor mite,' said Fern with easy sentimentality. 'Must be hard for her, losing her mum like that when she ain't got no father either.'

'Oh, I keeps an eye out for her, don't you worry. Mr Li takes an interest in that kid because she's half Chinese, and likes me to watch where she goes and who she talks to.'

'Pays you to grass on her, you mean,' said Fern scornfully. 'You don't never do nothing without you're paid for it, Jago, don't give me that bullshit.'

'Can't live on air,' muttered her brother as she pushed his head forward to cut curls clustering at the back of his neck.

It was true enough that he kept an eye on Candy, though this was less easy now she didn't accept pillion rides. Aunt Prue had forbidden them, and with the ever-present threat that she might be whisked away to London if she disobeyed, Candy trod carefully with her forceful aunt. Besides, the general hostility from Barleycourt stable staff made it inadvisable for Jago to spend time hanging about there. After finishing work at the Centre, however, he would tour the tracks through the woods on his scrambler bike with a pair of binoculars ready to take a close look at whatever or whoever was moving near the stables.

He knew their routines to a T. After evening stables, when the horses were hayed up, rugged up, and tucked up for the night, the yard central lights would be switched off; Johnny and Jeremy would cycle over the cattle grid and away to their tea; carrot-topped Seamus would take his quad bike off across the park, and last of all Helen Murray would give each loose box a final check, lock the tack room, and walk away through the big arch under the clock tower.

He could not predict with any certainty what she would do next. Sometimes the light would go on in the office she shared with Jonah in the front room of the big house, and Jago would guess she was dealing with accounts or telephoning clients. Sometimes a torch would shine across the gravel from the lodge, and he guessed that her father had joined her in the office. Jago was wary of her father. Down the pub he had heard a rumour that Martin Robb was a police officer – a DCI – on compassionate leave, which was enough to warn Jago to steer well clear. Better safe than sorry, he reminded himself.

'Penny for them?' said his sister, scissors poised. She pushed his head from side to side as she considered her work.

'Worth more'n that,' he grinned, and stood up, the black clippings cascading on to the lino. 'Give over, Fern. You've done enough. Where are those keys, now?'

Reluctantly she fetched her bag and handed them over. 'Don't you forget to top her up,' she warned.

'As if I would. Ta, sis.' A jingle of keys, a slammed door, and he was gone.

When will I ever learn? she thought ruefully.

*****

The frosty spell was followed, as it often is at the end of the year, by much warmer weather, midday temperatures in double figures, and strong westerlies that brought enough rain to please Fergal the huntsman, a number of whose bitch pack had been off games with sore pads. Good scenting conditions, too: word went round among subscribers that the Meet at Dukeshill Larches, hosted by Isabel Garraway, was likely to produce a good run, and every one of the Barleycourt livery owners signed on for it.

Robb had struck up a friendship with Jabez Crump, the older of the terriermen, a fearless cross-country navigator who worked for the local livestock auctioneers, and knew every byway and track in the neighbourhood that was negotiable by ATV. He was also a good agricultural carpenter, adept at patching up broken fences. Though it was rare, nowadays, for the services of a dog to be needed, a gate-shutting and fence-mending team to follow the Hunt and make running repairs was essential. Jabez was therefore a vital link in the hunting hierarchy, particularly since his extensive acquaintance with local farmers could give up-to-date information on where hounds would be welcome and where they should avoid.

'Stick to the high ground as far as you can,' advised Jonah, with the large-scale map spread over his desk at the briefing before the Dukeshill meet. Robb had been invited to sit in on the meeting and follow next day on Jabez's all-terrain vehicle. 'With ground as wet as this, no one's going to be keen on seventy times four hoofs churning up their winter pasture.'

Nods all round, then Jabez spoke up. 'Had a chat with old Enderby Wallis in the market last week. Seems he's gone out of sheep, and all his steers are housed by now, so he said he'd be glad to see us any time.'

'That's good of him,' said Jonah.

'And useful,' added Marjorie Whittle, who would be doubling the role of Field Master with her duties as Hunt Secretary. 'Once we get out of Dukeshill there's that big common – what's its name?'

'Kaley Common. Can't do no harm galloping there, and if the line goes down across that minor road and then up over Wallis's farm, you'll have plenty of timber fences to sort out your Field,' said Jabez with a grin. 'Here, take a look at the map.'

They all bent over it, exploring possibilities, finding back ways through villages, across streams, avoiding main roads; trying to guess the route their 'fox' – in the form of a super-fit cross-country runner – might take, and the ruses he might employ to throw hounds off the scent. The briefing took over an hour before everyone was satisfied that every angle had been covered.

'You mean this goes on before *every* hunt?' Robb asked Helen later that night, and she rolled her eyes.

'Has to. It's all so different nowadays, Dad. It's nearly twenty years since the Hunting Act was passed, and there are endless rules about what you can and can't do. We don't want to be reduced to a pack of two, like they are in Scotland, poor devils. Jonah and his Committee have worked out a pretty good relationship with the local police – we stick to the rules and so do they – but the sabs are a nuisance, always trying to catch hounds doing something they shouldn't but which they were bred for, which is of course hunting foxes.'

'Tricky,' agreed Robb.

'So we hunt a trail laid by a runner in an agreed area, but *if* hounds happen to find a fox and kill it instead, everyone agrees that it was an unfortunate accident. Mostly, of course, that doesn't happen,' she added hastily. 'Everyone has a lovely day in the fresh air and a lot of excitement, and everyone – except the poor frustrated huntsman – goes home happy. That's the theory, at least.'

'And the reality?'

Helen shrugged. 'Well, it makes us a living. But anyone who hunted before 2004 thinks it's a pretty poor substitute for the real thing, and they fly over to Ireland for a week of proper foxhunting on hirelings, going out with a different pack every day including Sundays. Noel promised to take me after Christmas when...' her voice cracked.

Baffled by emotion as always, Robb could only give her an awkward hug as she turned away to the sink and began washing up, but his determination to find out more about Jago's activities crystallised. If he was caught with wild foxes in his possession, he was surely guilty of an offence against the Hunting Act.

*****

Those who had predicted a good scenting day were proved right only minutes after hounds moved off. As usual, Isabel Garraway's meet had been a lavish affair, with nips of port-and-brandy brought round on silver salvers to diminish riders' perception of the size of the fences, and hot pies to fortify those who had sacrificed breakfast in order to be ready on time.

'Glorious!' sighed Jasmine Dymoke after her third thimbleful of jumping powder backed up by a sausage roll. 'I feel ready to take on Becher's now.'

Hunting two days a week for a month had much improved Betsinda's manners and calmed her so noticeably that today she wore no warning red – or even green – tail ribbon. She stood quietly while her rider laughed and chatted at the Meet, and half an hour later when hounds were thrown into covert only her rigid stance and sharply pricked ears showed that she knew precisely what the scuffling and whimpering, the crackling of dead bracken and occasional yelps meant.

'Nice little mare,' said a chatty stranger from a neighbouring Hunt eyeing her enviously. 'She'd just suit my daughter.'

Jasmine didn't answer. She was watching the far corner of the covert, where Harvey, the enthusiastic amateur whipper-in, mounted today on an immense piebald cob, had stationed himself between a stile and a low bank flanking a small pond. Standing up in his stirrups, he peered into the undergrowth where two or three hounds had congregated.

Suddenly one of them gave tongue, a deep positive bay that silenced the high yelps and yaps and brought the rest of the pack crashing and bounding towards the pond. A moment later they all owned the line with a spine-tingling chorus, streaming out of covert and across a ploughed field.

Harvey raised his hat high, and Fergal galloped down the grass ride bisecting the spinney, jumped the stile, and followed his pack, blowing the long, paper-tearing note of *Gone Away*.

Jasmine shortened her reins and turned Betsinda towards the stile. With a bound they were over, landing well clear of the first furrow, and following Fergal down the plough's wheel-track with the chatty stranger hot on their heels and the rest of the Field queueing for the stile. Mud was flying up in Betsinda's face and spattering Jasmine's coat, but although the plough itself was wet and heavy, the compacted wheel-track afforded relatively good going. They reached the far side of the field, clattered through a metal gate on to a lane, and turned sharply to face the high, flail-cut hedge, on the far side of which the pack was already streaming across a grass pasture.

The hedge was broad as well as high, and the run-up just a couple of strides. Fergal jumped clear; Harvey crashed through on his indomitable piebald cob, losing a stirrup-iron but recovering it quickly.

For a moment Jasmine was assailed by doubt. Would Betsinda face it? Was it fair to ask the little mare to jump such an obstacle straight off the road? But with the flagship hindquarters of her pal disappearing into the distance, Betsinda made up her rider's mind for her. Two strides, a neat-footed spring and hoist which sent her a foot beyond the limits of the hedge, and they were over in perfect unison, while a wave of pride warmed Jasmine's heart.

'Good girl!' she murmured, patting the mare's neck.

Meanwhile back at the covertside the big bay, Democrat, freshly clipped and leg trouble forgotten, was giving Ricky Owen a very rough ride.

'There are three kinds of fool,' his father had declared dogmatically at breakfast. 'There are fools, and there are bloody fools, and there are people who hunt in snaffles.'

He had regarded his son with disfavour tinged, it must be said, with a touch of jealousy for, a quarter of a century ago, Gervase Owen himself had been a very similar handsome, curly-haired, slim young man, able to fit into the beautifully tailored, made-to-measure hunt coat and mahogany-topped boots which Ricky would wear today. And now? The hair and the elegant figure were long gone, and only the conviction that things were done better in his day remained.

As with much of his father's advice, Ricky ignored this statement as old-fashioned tosh, but he did add a precautionary dropped noseband to Democrat's snaffle bridle, and was glad of it when the horse circled and jigged, refusing to stand quietly, making it clear that waiting round a wood on a wintry day was not his idea of hunting.

'Feeling his oats, is he?' said Jabez Crump with a laugh when Ricky took the stamping, fretting horse over to the quiet corner where Robb and Jabez were sharing a flask of coffee. 'Easy, boy. Easy.' He laid a hand on Democrat's rein. 'You'll get your fill of exercise soon if…' His voice changed and he stepped back sharply, 'Look out, they've found. Come on, Mr Robb, sir. Quick.'

Robb jumped aboard the ATV, which took off with a spray of muddy water which sent Democrat up on his hind legs. A couple of jarring bucks, and he was galloping to catch up with the rest of the Field, most of whom had negotiated one stile and were labouring over the field of heavy plough.

Two riders from the same stable who have travelled together to the Meet and stood beside one another at the first covert, can have such differing recollections of the day's events that they might have been out on different days.

For Jasmine and Betsinda this was a day of glory, a day to remember. Obstacles loomed up and were sailed over. Gates seemed to spring open the moment the little mare drew near. The cross-country runner had taken his brief seriously: twice in the first half hour hounds checked, puzzling out the line where he had run along a stream-bed, and again when he scaled a wall and jumped from the top into a barn full of farm machinery, where he rested a minute in the cab of a tractor before resuming his course.

After her good start, Jasmine was ahead of the rest of the Field when hounds checked, and was slightly irritated to find Mr Chatty close behind.

'You look as if you know what you're doing, so I stuck to you like glue,' he said. 'I say! That mare of yours goes like smoke and she can certainly jump. What'll you take for her?'

'She's not for sale,' said Jasmine, deciding to shake him off at the first opportunity, ignoring the well-known superstition that if you turn down an offer for a horse, something will go wrong with it before the month is out. Old wives' tales, thought Jasmine, crossing her fingers.

Fergal was casting his hounds forward into the field of stubble turnips where they had lost the scent, and the riders waited expectantly, with clouds of steam rising from the horses into the chilly air.

'I'm serious,' persisted Mr Chatty. He urged his hireling closer.

'Oh, rotten luck!' drawled a voice behind him, and he looked round. A well-upholstered woman on a sturdy roan patent-safety was pointing down at the hireling's off fore. 'You can't go on like that.'

'Damn and blast!' Mr Chatty dismounted and surveyed the damage. The hireling's off-fore shoe had twisted, yanking out most of the clenches, but the remaining nails were still too firmly fixed for him to pull the shoe off by hand. After a couple of tries he gave up.

'Must have been that sticky plough,' he said disconsolately. 'Where can I find a farrier?'

Riders crowded round, offering advice, and Jasmine edged away. Fergal, his horse knee-deep in stubble turnips, was cheering on the bulk of the pack through the middle of the field, but far to his left a small party of hounds, with Harvey monitoring them, was making an independent investigation on the left-hand headland, where a wide strip had been left unsown.

As Jasmine watched the headland, she glimpsed a ginger streak steal out from the turnip leaves and disappear into the rough grass, so quickly that she had to blink to be sure she'd seen it. Harvey had too. Silently he raised his cap, but at the same moment hounds hit off the cross-country runner's trail on the far side of the stubble.

'*Yow-yow-yow!*' The deep, bell-like tone of a senior hound brought the gossiping Field to attention.

'Hark to Dambuster!'

Doubling his horn in short rapid notes, Fergal galloped to where the ever-reliable Dambuster was owning the line, bringing the rest of the pack leaping and scuffling through the wet leaves in a compact tri-coloured stream. They burst out of the turnips on a breast-high scent with a tremendous cry which quite drowned out the more tentative tongue of the five independent investigators the other side of the field.

Away went Fergal and the trail followers, together with the bulk of the riders, and away in the other direction went the five independent hounds with Harvey labouring through the wet turnips to catch up and whip them off the line of a real live fox. His cob was not built for speed though, and was carrying several pounds' weight of clay clinging to each of his stubby legs: to his chagrin, Jasmine and light-footed Betsinda flew past him on the headland after the rapidly disappearing fivesome.

'Stay with them!' he gasped, pummelling the cob's sides. 'I'll catch you up.'

Some hope! Betsinda had the bit between her teeth and Jasmine could not have stopped her even if she wanted to. The line taken by the fox was very different from the sanitised, horse-friendly route so carefully chosen by the cross-country runner. He was a travelling dog-fox who had been seeking both dinner and a mate among the duck ponds of the local Shoot. After a night of passion he had been lying up with the remains of his meal when he heard Fergal's horn and decided to make himself scarce. Once into the wood flanking the turnip field, he trotted unhurriedly between clumps of brambles on his well-worn route home, breaking into a lope only when the clamour of his pursuers sounded too close behind him.

Guided by their cry, Jasmine brought Betsinda under control and followed into the wood, weaving a path under low-hanging branches until she reached a forestry track, where huge vehicles like metal dinosaurs had dragged out timber and were parked in a clearing. The cry of the few hounds sticking to their fox was fainter now, but she rode towards it along the track which, although punctuated by long puddles, was at least better going than the unthinned wood. Where was everyone else? she wondered. Where – if anywhere – is this leading?

The track branched, and she chose the less churned-up arm because it seemed to be where her little pack was heading, but after half a mile or so it branched again and again, reducing first to grass and then to a mere thread of path, and now her worry crystallised into whether she would ever find the way back or along the path, or be doomed to wander about this wood until her horse collapsed with exhaustion. Not that Betsinda showed any sign of tiredness yet. On the contrary she picked her way neatly, stepping over fallen logs and skirting heaps of brashings. When she drew rein to stand and listen, Jasmine realised that the sound of hunting had stopped completely.

An explosion of pheasants clattered into the air, and when their indignant cocking-up was gone, complete stillness seemed to settle over the wood. She strained her ears for a distant horn, the thud of hoofs, even a whimper or yap, but there was nothing. She was alone.

As usual at such inconvenient moments, a pressing desire to pee came over her. The idea of struggling with zips and buttons was unattractive, but on the other hand, when would she get a better opportunity than this? It might be hours before she had another chance. She had nothing but the reins with which to tether Betsinda so would have to trust her not to break them and make off. Hurriedly she buckled them round a low branch on an ivy-covered tree that had fallen at a slant across the path, with the upper limbs suspended on its neighbours, stripped off the necessary layers – breeches, long johns, tights and pants – and crouched down.

It was just as she was replacing the layers that she happened to look up into the ivy above her head and saw a sharp, anxious face with pricked ears gazing down at her. For a long moment they stared at one another.

'OK, Charlie. You're safe there,' she murmured, hastily completing her dressing. The fox did not move. Quietly, cautiously she rose, untied Betsinda and rode away.

*****

Robb's teeth felt loose in their sockets when Jabez at last slowed down long enough for his passenger to get out and fasten the chain round an elaborate wrought iron gate. Ordinary gates he dealt with from the ATV's driving seat, yanking them brutally into position and clicking the catch, but Isabel Garraway's Meet had been held on the back lawn of her big house with the garden gate opened specially to act as a filter through which members of the Hunt and possible troublemakers could be kept apart.

'No sense in making things easy for that noisy lot,' said Jabez, nodding towards Fern and her party of banner-waving sabs.

STOP TORTURING FOXES! urged the banners. BAN HUNTING!

'Don't worry, they can't keep up with horses,' he added. 'Gate secure? Right, all aboard, then,' and off he roared again, following the separate pocked trails of hoofprints across a series of inviting stubbles that showed where bold spirits had flown over the fences while more prudent souls sought out gates.

In the back of the ATV Jabez carried hammer and nails, staples and wire, crowbar and mallet besides some solid fence posts – all the tools needed for running repairs to hedges, walls and gates that had suffered from the cavalry charge.

'Patch 'em up and make them stockproof. That's all we need do now,' he told Robb. 'I'll be back later in the week with my mate to make a proper job of it.' As the vehicle bounced over furrows and hillocks the tools banged and clattered, making it hard to hear one another speak and Robb gripped the safety handle until his knuckles whitened.

For a couple of hours they followed, working steadily as the hunt moved ahead of them, shutting gates, repairing stiles, closing gaps in hedges with a bar and a couple of new posts, before stopping in a sunny patch beside a haystack for cheese sandwiches and a flask of tea from a knapsack.

Jabez was a talker. 'Shame about your son-in-law,' he began confidentially, busy with a roll-up. 'One of the best, he was. You don't get to see many like him, not in this day and age.'

Robb made an indeterminate noise, then said, 'I hardly knew him. They were married such a short time.'

Jabez looked sceptical. 'Bit of a rumpus over that, eh? According to what I heard.'

'You could say that,' agreed Robb cautiously, wondering where this was leading.

Where it was leading was to an incendiary diatribe against former racehorse trainer Norrie MacAleese. His morals, his manners, his mates, his fraudulent dealing in livestock, his dirty tricks, his blatant lying. 'Had it in for Mr Noel, didn't he? Ever since he lost his licence he wanted to get his own back and wouldn't listen to reason.'

'What did Noel have to do with that?'

Jabez looked crafty. 'I don't say he did and I don't say he didn't, but there's some as will tell you that him and his brother had a quiet word with the Stewards. Jockey Club Stewards, that is. Them as runs racing. Told them that horses from MacAleese's yard weren't running true to form and they ought to look into why. That set the cat among the pigeons, right enough, and when old Norrie lost his licence he began to ask who'd been blabbing.'

Robb digested this information. He said, 'My daughter told me it was a – a disagreement over a horse that Noel sold him.'

'Ah, that's something else entirely,' Jabez took a drag at his roll-up. 'but it's part of the same thing. Take that horse he bought against all advice – the one your daughter told you about. I told him – the vet told him – and Mr Noel told him time and again that he had a heart murmur, but because Norrie had a buyer lined up, one of those Arabs with money to burn but who could turn on a sixpence and deny that he'd ever promised to buy, he wouldn't listen…'

Robb chewed his sandwich and let the intricacies of who said what to whom wash over him. The story might be opaque but it was perfectly clear that Noel and Norrie MacAleese had been at odds for a long time.

'But what about Anne Cutler?' he cut in. 'Don't forget it was *her* car. Why should anyone booby-trap that?'

'Ah, little Anne!' When Jabez smiled his leathery cheeks became a mass of curved lines. 'She was the quiet one. When I worked for her Dad – before his troubles caught up with him – she was the prettiest little thing you ever saw. The sister did all the talking, she was a great one to talk, and Anne kept everything to herself, except when she wanted something. The father spoiled those girls rotten, but their ma used to try to make them do a bit of work. 'Plait up my pony for me, *please,*

Jabez,' little Anne used to say. 'I can't get it right and Mummy will be so cross.' Twist me round her little finger, she could, and nine times out of ten it was because she wanted her pony to beat Isabel Garraway's. That was the one thing she cared about, getting the better of Isabel.'

'Did the Cutler family stay in the village when the father was gaoled?'

'Sold the house, sold the livestock, and off they went to London. I'm told Anne got a helping hand from an uncle in the Far East – or was it Hong Kong? – and lived in those parts while the older girl trained at some college. We never saw hide nor hair of them until Anne came back a couple of years ago and started working at that Chinese school. You'd never have thought she'd be the one to earn her living, and the daughter's half Chinese, I'd say. Ah, it's a funny old world.' He pinched out his roll-up and got to his feet. 'Now, sir, if you've had enough o' that, we'd best be up and doing.'

The Hunt had moved on, but Jabez knew exactly where to find them. Robb spotted a few stragglers first, then the bulk of the Field could be seen on the far side of an enormous expanse of plough, in which an accommodating farmer had left two wide headlands and a strip of grass down the middle. Bunched together, the riders were taking it in turns to jump the triangle of bars known as a tiger trap since the rest of the high hedge was reinforced with barbed wire.

'Trouble over there!' shouted Jabez, veering sharply towards the right-hand hedge, in which was a gaping hole. Through it they could see a girl on an unclipped pony whose coat was black with sweat trying to catch a loose horse, while on the ground, half in and half out of the ditch, lay an ominously still figure.

As the ATV drew up to him, he stirred and tried to sit up before collapsing back in the ditch.

It was not Ricky Owen's day.

'Wire,' he mumbled through a mouthful of mud. 'My legs are caught.'

Out came Jabez's wirecutters, snipping away at the rusty tangle that trapped him, while Robb went over to help the girl who had succeeded in catching Democrat's rein.

'Shall I take him?'

'Oh, yes, please.'

With relief she handed over the big horse, waved her thanks, and was away at a smart canter before Robb had a chance to protest. Democrat made a spirited attempt to follow her, but Robb pulled the reins over his head and, holding them in an iron grip, led him back to the hole in the fence where he found Jabez giving Ricky a piece of his mind.

'Maybe that'll learn you to look before you leap, young man. D'you think I spend my Sundays building tiger traps so's you can jump barbed wire not fifty yards away? That horse of yourn could have been cut to ribbons.' He inspected the broken ends of wire, and added, 'Good job there's no stock in here, or we'd have been jiggered.'

Ricky made no attempt to avoid the onslaught, but said meekly, 'I know. I was a fool. Thanks for pulling me out. I thought I was there for keeps.' He walked unsteadily to where Robb was holding Democrat and tried to get his foot in the stirrup.

'Wait a bit. Who's the prime minister?' demanded Jabez.

'Mrs Thatcher.'

'Ah, yes, of course. And I'm the Queen of Sheba.' His mouth turned down. 'Sorry, young man, but you're not getting back on that horse. Not just yet.'

'But I'm perfectly all right. I feel fine. Promise.'

'All the same, you're coming for a little ride along of me. Now don't argue, get aboard.' He hustled the still-protesting

Ricky into the passenger seat and said to Robb, 'Follow that line of trees to the end of the field and you'll find a little stone bridge with a gate on to the road. OK? Will you ride or walk?'

Robb looked with some misgiving at the over-excited bay, and said firmly, 'I'll walk.'

'Right. I'll ring Barleycourt as soon as I can get a signal, and ask them to send someone to collect the horse. You can hitch a lift."

With the white-faced Ricky now beginning to shiver with reaction, he started the engine and drove slowly away across the field.

'Right, boy,' said Robb to Democrat, patting his neck. 'Now behave yourself. Looks like we're in for a long walk.'

# CHAPTER SIX

WITH TWO CUTS and a colouring job booked before she modelled for a life-drawing class at midday, Fern was up early and dressed with particular care. Customer No 1 would be Isabel Garraway – *Miss* Garraway, as she liked to be called – whose fine blonde flyaway hair was a nightmare to cut, but whose lavish tips could be relied on.

Peering from the bedroom window, she was pleased to see her little green van parked in its usual place.

Good boy, she thought. Looks like he's given it a wash, too. *And* put the key through the letterbox like I asked him to: wonders will never cease.

The black bag loaded with hairdressing equipment swung from her shoulder as she opened the driver's door and hefted it on to the passenger seat, but the moment she took a breath inside she recoiled, gagging.

'What the *hell's* that stink?'

A horrible feral smell that mingled ammonia, exhaust fumes and floral air freshener pervaded the whole vehicle, making it impossible to breathe without choking.

Furious, she jumped out, grabbing her mobile, stabbing buttons. 'You little shit!' she screamed at her brother. 'What you been doing with my car? Come on, I want the truth. It smells unbelievable, like – like the elephant house at the zoo.'

'Cool it, sis. I'm not deaf.' Jago was all injured innocence. 'I done just what you said – filled the tank and then me and Rube spent half the night washing out that car of yours.'

'But the smell! It's horrible. I can't go visiting my ladies in a car that stinks to high heaven.'

'It don't smell no more.' said Jago doggedly. 'Not so's you'd notice.'

'It bloody does. What is it, anyway?'

He was silent, and she said impatiently, 'Come on, I want to know, and I'm going to go on asking until you come clean. If you ever hope to *borrow* my car again…'

'Foxes,' he said sullenly.

'*What?*' Again her voice rose to a scream. 'You telling me you put *foxes* in my van? Are you mad?'

'Now look, sis, this here's the long and short of it.' Jago's voice was all sweet reason. 'There's a family in London, nice family, that's bin driven outa their mind by foxes under their rockery. Killed their cat, dug out the kids' rabbits and tossed them about the lawn; dog got fox mange, pest control couldn't help…'

'So they paid you to take them away in my van, eh? A likely tale,' she said with heavy irony. 'How did you get them into it? Tell me that. Opened the back door and said, "Walk in"?'

'You've got it all wrong,' he protested. 'I done them a favour. Taken their foxes somewhere they could be free, just like you're always goin' on about with them sabs.'

'Don't tell me those foxes are free now.' Fern could put two and two together and she knew her brother. 'You gassed them in my car, didn't you? That's why it stinks of exhaust.'

'Only the big 'uns. The cubs are free, like I said.' He sniggered. 'You might find your posh Miss Garraway chasing them little uns instead of that trail they've laid, and what will the cops say to that, eh?'

Fern was silent, thinking this out.

'Gotta go. Cheers, sis.'

'Wait one. You just tell me what you done with all these dead foxes. Tipped them out at the first roundabout, for the binmen to pick up, eh? What if someone saw you and took your number. My number? I could get in a lotta trouble for that.'

'Tipped 'em out? You're joking.' Jago was scornful. 'The Chinks pay good money for fox skins. They've killed all their own wild ones and foxes bred in cages have patchy pelts, hardly worth the skinning.'

'And who does the skinning?'

His silence answered the question.

'You disgust me, Jags. You really do. And I can tell you one more thing, you won't be borrowing my van again in a hurry, no matter how you beg and plead, so don't go thinking you'll get me to change my mind because that's not going to happen.'

She tied a scarf over her hair and drove to the Grange with all the windows open, and Jago was right: by the time she got there she was no longer conscious of the smell. She refused the butler's offer to carry her equipment bag, and made her way to the big bathroom with its dressing table and triple mirror, where she laid out the tools of her trade and tidied her windblown hair, hoping that Miss Garraway would be on time for once.

Faintly she could hear the familiar high, little-girl voice complaining about a missed delivery and she grinned, glad that someone else was getting it in the neck; but when at length Isabel drifted in through the bathroom door, it was plain that her morning had not been going well.

'Ah, there you are at last,' she said, as if Fern had been keeping her waiting. 'No time for a wash today, so you can run that basin out again. Goodness knows why I employ all these people and they can't sort out the smallest problem without coming running to me.'

She gave an exasperated sigh, plonking herself in front of the mirror and turning her head this way and that. 'All I need today is a trim, to look respectable for the Hunt Ball. So level up the ends, will you, and check the layers until Antoine comes over from New York and gives me a proper cut at the end of the month. Damp it down, there's a good girl, and I'll show you how I want it to look...'

Fern bit her lip. A trim for someone as demanding as Miss Garraway took just as long as a cut, but she could charge only half. Like all home stylists she could chat away on auto-pilot while concentrating on the work in hand, and she listened with half an ear to Isabel's stream-of-consciousness musings about her plans for dressage competitions and horse sales, social gatherings and hunt balls, none of which meant a thing to her; snipping away industriously until stopped by an electrifying screech.

'*No, no, no!* Antoine goes mad if anyone touches my fringe! Leave it longer at the sides, like I said. Look! *This* bit's got to tuck behind my ears. Silly girl! You've cut it much too short and now it'll stick out without hairspray.'

Who's doing this trim, you or me? thought Fern mutinously. Miss Garraway was silent for a couple of minutes while Fern tried to strike a balance between the too-short right side and too-long left, but it was a losing battle.

'Oh, leave it. That'll do,' she exclaimed impatiently, to Fern's relief. 'It's a perfectly simple style – I can't understand why you make such a fuss about getting it right. If Antoine could see me now, he'd have a fit.' She paused, then said in a different tone, 'By the way, what's that appalling smell? I think it's coming from your bag.'

'Must be the chemicals I use for colouring,' said Fern uneasily, hoping Miss Garraway would not take a fancy to investigate further. 'Some of them are really strong. Dangerous. I have to wear gloves when I handle them.'

'What people will risk to improve their appearance!' Isabel moved her head to left and right then used a hand mirror to inspect the back. 'Do you know, they used to eat *arsenic* to make their hair shine? And paint their faces with white lead? All the same, I think the sooner you take that bag away the better. I don't want my cleaner giving notice.'

Fern was glad to escape – glad, too, of the £20 note added to her fee – but still furious with her brother for his treatment of her van, wondering how she could get even with him.

So he sold the skins of the adult foxes to the Chinese people he worked for. That was clear enough. What he hadn't explained was what happened to the fox cubs he left to fend for themselves. Where did he put them? Did he feed them? Were they old enough to hunt for themselves?

In her easy, sentimental way, Fern loved TV documentaries about wild animals and the thought of those abandoned fox cubs bothered her for the rest of her working day. Collecting her chicken takeaway from the pub window just before he closed at five, she impulsively asked Mario the publican if he had any carcases to spare for a soup, and was rewarded with an astonished laugh and the offer of a dozen.

'That enough?' he asked with his gap-toothed grin. 'Glad to be rid of them. Binmen always complain they attract rats if I put them out with the black bags.'

She thanked him and he called, 'Come back tomorrow if you want any more.'

Now to decide where to distribute this largesse. Fern drove slowly along the single-track road that skirted the surrounding wall of the Confucius Centre, hoping to meet her brother on his way home. No luck, but when she pulled into one of the passing-places to call him, he answered at once.

'Hi, sis. Got over your grumps yet?'

'Look, Jago, I want to know where you put those fox cubs. I been thinking about them all day. If you don't tell me where to find them, I'm going to report you to the RSPCA.'

'Go on. You wouldn't.'

'Like to bet?'

'Anyways, you'll never find 'em now,' he blustered. 'Cubs are good at hiding.'

'Tell me where you put them or I'll report you.'

He gave up, as she knew he would. 'Oh, all right. If you're set on busting a gut looking for those cubs, I can't stop you, but I warn you it's no good. You're never gonna find them in that wood.'

'Which wood?'

'Hamber's Spinney,' he said sulkily. 'Tipped 'em outa the bags right on the edge of the common where the Hunt's gonna draw first on Thursday. Likely they'll be miles away by now.'

We'll see about that, she thought, breaking the connection. The smell of roast chicken hardened her resolve. Poor little things, they must be so hungry! It was only a couple of miles to Hamber's Spinney, and there by the gate that led into the wood were recent tyre tracks where a car – her van, no doubt – had driven in, reversed, and driven out again.

For a moment her resolve faltered at the prospect of walking through the mud in unsuitable shoes, but she pushed away the urge to retreat. Getting out of the van, she opened the gate wide then drove through, wheels skidding on wet turf, and parked facing the hedge where it could not be seen from the road. She shut the gate, took the bag of carcases from the back, and set off into the wood.

*****

On the shoulder of the hill above, Jabez loaded his tools into the ATV and stood back to survey his handiwork. A nice job of patching up, he thought. Almost as good as new.

A movement in the field below caught his eye and he picked up his binoculars for a closer look at the green van being driven through the road gate. Who the hell? This was private land. No one had the right to park in Hamber's Spinney; certainly not the tall woman with improbably orange hair now emerging from the driver's door. A figure that was vaguely familiar. Wasn't she one of those banner-waving sabs? What was she doing here?

Full of curiosity, he watched as she took a plastic shopping-bag from the van and made her way into the wood, turning frequently to stare about her as if looking for something. The middle ride was marked with many hoofprints, being a favourite with local riders, and he guessed that the mud would soon deter her from further exploration.

Sure enough, in ten minutes she reappeared, swinging the bag, and hurried to the van. That ground's soft, reflected Jabez. She'll get stuck, sure as eggs, if she don't give it a good bit of welly through the gate.

He was right. Once she had stopped to pull it open and tried to restart, the wheels spun uselessly. Despite frantic revving, the vehicle slid sideways into the gatepost where it stuck fast.

Damned if I'm going down there to pull her out, he thought, continuing to pick up his tools. Far as I'm concerned she can stop there all night; but by the time he was ready to leave, a last look through binoculars showed that two men had joined the redhead, and were trying to shove the van back to the road.

One had the driver's door open and was steering as he pushed. The girl and the second man – tall, black-haired, and also familiar – were shoving from behind but without success. The van remained wedged against the gatepost.

Gestures and body language indicated a flaming row between all three. 'Bit of argy-bargy going on there,' diagnosed Jabez, wondering whether to reverse his earlier decision and lend them his spade.

He watched as the men spread sacks and a tarpaulin in front of the van, reversed a few yards on to firmer ground, and attached a rope to the front bumper. With the free end tied to the carrier of a motorbike on which the men must have arrived, the scene was set for a final effort. By now more cars had stopped to enjoy the show: he counted four men and six women in the little crowd gathered at the roadside.

'One...two...three...*heave!*' he imagined them chanting.

The green van shot forward, hit the soft patch again, the connecting rope strained for a long moment, then manpower triumphed. The van was back on the road, the gate closed, sacks and tarpaulin folded and stowed.

As the audience melted away, Jabez took a long, close look at the bikers who had come to the redhead's aid, and filed it away in his memory. Tall, black-haired Daniel 'Corky' O'Sullivan, last seen in a magistrate's court being bound over to keep the peace after a punch-up during a demo; and Jago Smith, groundsman to the Confucius Centre in Dorningdale and brother of Miss Garraway's hairdresser, Fern. Yes, he would know them again.

*****

'Look! No hands!' Fresh from a session with his physio, Jonah walked cautiously but unsupported across the office and sat down at his desk.

Helen clapped. 'Bravo! How does it feel?'

'Pretty insecure, to be honest. But Maksym says it's high time I stopped relying on my crutch.'

She pulled a face. 'Maksym's a bully.'

'A very handsome, very fit bully,' he agreed. 'Still, I suppose he knows best, and that's what I pay him for. Where's your father?'

'Taking Gus for a ride in Jabez Crump's ATV. He likes it even more than Seamus' tractor. They've gone to fetch some more fence posts from the woodyard.'

Jonah smiled. 'That's good, because I want to have a serious talk with you. Now, come on, Hels. Don't start shaking your head when you haven't heard what I'm going to say.'

'I can guess. And the answer is No.'

'I warn you I'm going to go on asking until I get the answer I want.'

'Then we can look forward to some pretty boring conversations,' she said sharply, turning back to her computer.

He picked up the telephone and made a couple of calls before returning to the attack. 'Hels…'

'No.' She gave an exasperated sigh. 'Don't you understand? I can't. I don't want to, and no matter how much you nag I'm not going to.'

'What I really don't understand is why you're so set on isolating yourself and making yourself miserable when you know it's the last thing my brother would have wanted.'

'How do you know what he would have wanted?'

'Because we had a pact.'

'What does that mean?'

'Just that we planned what to do about this place…' his gesture encompassed the house, the buildings, the land – 'if one of us was killed, and we both agreed to it. That was when Noel was mad about skydiving and I had just started on this racing game, so the odds of one or other getting damaged were pretty high. The long and short of what we agreed was that if he died in a bad landing or I broke my neck, the survivor would not sell up but would carry on with the business and running the estate just as before. No matter what it cost.'

She regarded him thoughtfully. Because it was rare for Jonah to speak seriously about personal matters she had never realised how deep was his attachment to Barleycourt or how strong his determination to preserve it.

'Of course we thought it would never happen. Hoped it wouldn't, or at least not for many years. But now it has, and the pact Noel and I made still applies. I shall do my damnedest to avenge my brother and find out who killed him, but until then I must just keep going, hold the place together, and to do that I'm going to need your help.'

'I don't see how coercing me into coming to the Hunt Ball is going to help you in any way,' she objected. 'I don't want to go, and that's all there is to it. It's too soon. I should hate every minute and ruin the party for everyone else.'

'Rubbish,' he said cheerfully. 'The only thing that would spoil the party would be for you to duck out of it. How are your friends going to feel thinking of you sitting brooding at home while they enjoy themselves? Dora Marshall's coming, though you could argue that she has as much reason as you not to feel in a party mood. Besides, I've an ulterior motive: I just know Isabel will step up pressure on me to let her redecorate my whole house unless you are there to protect me.'

She couldn't help laughing. 'Don't tell me you're frightened of Isabel.'

'Of course I am. We all are. Once she sets her mind on something she's unstoppable. She's been nagging me for years about holes in carpets and curtains falling to bits.' Voices and footsteps outside interrupted him. 'Ah, here's the fencing party back. Let's see if your father can talk some sense into you.'

Oh, for heaven's sake, leave me alone! she thought. Let me grieve as I want to. But Jonah's endless good nature stopped her saying it aloud and besides a tiny doubt was growing in her mind. It had seemed the proper, most appropriate course to hide herself away after such a bereavement, to refuse invitations and wallow in her sorrow; yet here was Jonah, who had lost a brother, arguably the most important person in his life and certainly the one he loved most, fully prepared to put his feelings to one side and carry on smiling. Shouldn't she do the same?

'Hels –?'

'I'll think about it,' she said in a muffled voice, hair swinging forward to hide her face as she bent over the computer. 'Now give me a break, please, and let me concentrate. If I don't get these accounts sent off today, there'll be no money coming in until after Christmas and no forage deliveries either, so you'll have a lot of hungry horses to add to your problems.'

'Can't risk that,' he agreed, and if there was the faintest note of satisfaction in his tone it was impossible for her to detect.

*****

Jago counted Mr Li's notes with care before folding them in a tight wad and stuffing them in his back pocket. He said, 'Six fox pelts on those boards plus two squirrels. What about paying for the squirrels?'

Mr Li made a dismissive gesture that indicated squirrel skins were worth nothing.

'So I'll take them back, OK?'

But when Jago bent to remove the squirrel skins from the board, Mr Li said quickly,

'Leave them. I think of someone who will buy the skins of squirrels. I pay – ah – six pounds for two.'

Proper old skinflint, thought Jago. Still, it was better than nothing. He had added the squirrel skins on spec, but wouldn't bother with them in future. They were hardly worth the trouble of skinning.

He added the cash to his pocket and said casually, 'I been keeping an eye on the Cutler girl, like you said. Seen who she talks to and so on.'

Mr Li's expression did not change, but Jago sensed his interest sharpen.

'Not so easy now they don't need me to look after her ponies,' he added. 'Price of fuel's gone up, and that aunt of hers keeps a close eye on her. Proper tartar, she is, an' all.'

'Tell me what you have seen,' said Mr Li curtly, and Jago realised he could not spin it out any further.

'She goes riding and meets a Chinese fellow in the woods, that's all. Not for long, and he's not one of yours from this place.'

'What does he look like, this Chinese man?'

Jago shrugged. 'I ain't never seen him close to, but he's tall, and wears a hat with a wide brim. Could be anyone.'

'How do you know he's Chinese?'

'She bows to him, that's how.'

Mr Li considered this, and said, 'Where do they meet?'

'Loads of different places.' Jago wasn't going to make this easy. 'Up on the common; in the woods; at a crossroad. Sometimes he comes on a bike, sometimes on foot. You gotta watch where she goes, and get ahead and take care she doesn't see you or she'll warn him not to show up.' He anticipated Mr Li's next question. 'Got her phone with her, ain't she? Gives him a buzz and tells him to keep away.'

'Ah.' Mr Li considered for a moment, then said, 'You will show the meeting places to Hu Jinxiao, so that he may speak to this man.'

Speak to? More likely beat him up, thought Jago, who had in the past witnessed the shaven-headed gatekeeper's methods of interrogation of unwanted visitors.

He said, 'I told you, it's not that easy to get close to them. You'd better wait until I spot him and tell you where to come. May take a while on top of my regular work, and I'll need paying.'

'You will be paid.'

'Say a hundred pounds. That should cover it. Time, fuel, and so on.'

'Fifty.'

They compromised on £85; and Jago sauntered off well satisfied because he already knew perfectly well where the next meeting was to be.

*****

Thursday morning, rain sluicing down in the yard behind The Feathers, horses with tails tucked in against the east wind, and only the hardiest of the hardcore Hunt members determined to enjoy what promised to be a very wet day.

'Not a sign of a sab,' said Jabez to Robb, wiping his nose with the back of his hand as he clambered into the ATV.

'Just as well, too. Between you and me I had to shoot three fox cubs in Hamber's Spinney yesterday. Starving, they were, and shivering with cold. That fool woman had been trying to feed them chicken bones. I saw her at it and thought I'd best see what was goin' on.'

'What fool woman?'

'Tall one with ginger hair. You saw her at the Garraway meet last week. The one waving a banner and screaming.'

Robb recognised the description. 'Oh, her.'

'Beats me how she knew where those cubs were,' ruminated Jabez.

Time to put cards on the table, thought Robb. He said, 'She knew because her brother put them there.'

Jabez looked shocked. 'Get away!'

'He fetches them from London – doped, I imagine – kills the adults and sells the skins to the Chinese he works for, then puts out the cubs for the Hunt to find. He's got quite a business going. '

'The dirty dog,' said Jabez with deep disapproval. 'And how do you come to know all this?'

'Picked up bits and pieces here and there,' said Robb vaguely. 'Look out, they're off.'

As they puttered along in the wake of the Field, Jabez said worriedly, 'Trouble is, I can't be sure I got all those cubs. Someone ought to warn Fergal.'

'I told Jonah Murray what I suspected was happening. '

Jabez looked relieved. 'Ah, that's all right, then. If Mr Jonah knows, he'll soon put a stop to it. And Miss Garraway will go mad when she hears what that boy's been up to, right under her nose, and she a magistrate, too.'

'What do you mean? I thought he worked for the Confucius Centre.'

'Ah, so he does, but he lives in that brick cottage by Miss Garraway's old walled garden. Gardener's Cottage, they call it. His dad was her dad's head gardener, and when old Gregory died, she let Jago Smith go on renting.'

For a few minutes they sat in silence, the rain trickling under their hats and between collar and shirt. 'Shoulda put the cover on her today,' Jabez mused. 'Cuts down visibility, though, on a day like this.'

Once on the move, though, the dozen riders were warm enough, the half-ton of horse under each of them acting as a giant hot-water bottle, and the mixed emotions of excitement and fear sending adrenalin levels soaring.

'Looks like we're heading for Lover's Leap,' called Jasmine to Candy, who was having difficulty restraining Fireball from forcing his way past her to the front.

Side by side, they jostled through a gate, crossed a strip of grass and faced up to the celebrated Leap, which required a plunge off a grassy bank bold enough to clear the deep water undercutting the bank and reach the mid-stream shallows of the Connor Brook. A couple of splashy strides were then followed by a sharp scramble up the opposite bank which quickly turned into a mudslide.

At times like these, Candy regretted more than ever the loss of Little Orchid, who never took flying leaps without careful consideration, and had often dealt with this particular obstacle by sitting on his tail and sliding into the water, wading gently through the deep stream until he reached the shallows, and scrabbling his way up the mudslide as a mule does, with his nose on the ground and a leg or two to spare.

Fireball, however, tackled it in a very different way, with such an exaggerated spring on take-off that he landed in the water with a tremendous splash and Candy halfway up his neck.

'Hang on to his mane,' called Jasmine, leaning over perilously from her own horse to catch the girl by the shoulder, and heaving her back into the saddle.

On the bank, Jabez was laughing. 'Anne's kid missed a ducking there! That pony of hers is a bit hot for hunting, but she rides well. I've seen her in the woods once or twice lately, talking to a tall bloke. Chinese by the looks of him.' He gave Robb a sideways glance. 'How are you coppers getting on with your investigation, eh? Found anything to link old Norrie to the car bomb?'

'His alibi looks rock solid, I'm afraid.'

'Ah, well.' Jabez shook his head regretfully. 'Hunt Ball coming up but it won't be the same without Mr Noel to do the auction. He was the one to make a party go. Good as a play, it was, to hear him bidding up Miss Garraway for summat she'd didn't want, both of them laughing their heads off and the money rolling in.'

'Jonah's trying to persuade my daughter to go with him,' observed Robb, and Jabez nodded vigorously.

'So she should. So she should. 'Tain't no use sitting moping at home – won't do no good to no one. Glad to see her out on her horse today, at all events. Nothing like a gallop to blow away the cobwebs.'

It was the first time since her husband's death that Helen had ridden to hounds, and she had deliberately picked a day when few people would be out. The client who had hired her black mare, Lucky Dip, had pulled out after seeing the weather forecast, and on the spur of the moment Helen decided to ride her herself. It was a relief that everyone treated her as if nothing had happened to change her whole life, and as the familiar pattern of the day unfolded even she had to remind herself how different things were now from the last time – and would always be without Noel. No longer need she hoard the memory of every incident, however small, that they could laugh over together, even if every field, covert, jump still reminded her of her loss. With no difficulty she could imagine Noel's comments on the looks and performance of every horse and rider and add those of her own but it seemed pointless if they could not be shared with him.

Nevertheless, as Lucky Dip's powerful haunches launched them smoothly over the fences their trail-layer had chosen, she had to acknowledge that however guilty it made her feel, she was enjoying taking part in the day's sport again.

Both Robb and Jonah noted her improved mood that evening but forebore to comment. Candy had no such inhibitions. 'You and Lucky looked marvellous today,' she said admiringly. 'Everyone was so glad to see you again.'

Helen said nothing, but a little glow touched the hard, cold lump in her heart.

Candy rattled on: 'Did you see what Fireball did at the Lovers' Leap? I thought I was a goner. If Jasmine hadn't caught me I'd have come off bang in the middle of the stream. I'm starving, Hels. Can I have two boiled eggs for tea, to get back my energy?'

\*\*\*\*\*

Two days before the Hunt Ball, thick fog blanketed the Barleycourt woods, but by eleven it had begun to clear. Everyone was too busy helping and hindering the team erecting the big marquee in the park to notice Candy saddling Fireball and heading into the spinney known as Holly Grove – everyone, that is, except Jago, who waited for girl and pony to disappear into the tall beeches, then rang Mr Li.

'You know that bloke you wanted to talk to?' he said without preamble. 'Well, she's gone to meet him now. Yes. Right now. It'll take her half an hour to get to the rendezvous, so you've plenty of time to reach it first.'

'Where will she meet him?'

'In the woods. Got a pencil? The W3W's Snuggle. Carp. Melon. Put those words in the satnav and it'll take you right to the spot.'

'You have shown this place to Mr Hu?'

Jago's differences of opinion with the shaven-headed gatekeeper often ended in a scuffle, and he reckoned he was more likely to get paid if Mr Li himself was fully involved.

'Didn't seem to understand what I was on about,' he lied glibly. 'You best handle it yourself. All you need to find them are those words I just given you, and listen: I don't want the girl getting hurt. Wait until she leaves before you tackle the bloke.'

'The girl will come to no harm,' said Mr Li stiffly. 'Struggle. Carp. Melon.'

'*Snuggle* not Struggle.'

'Snuggle. Carp. Melon.'

'You got it. Cheers.'

Jago broke the connection and sat on his motorbike, bitter thoughts gnawing at him. He was still burning with resentment after his interview with Isabel Garraway. Boot him out of the snug little cottage and sheds he had fixed up at his own expense, would she? He'd see about that. He'd soon get even with that high-handed bitch who thought she could order everyone about just because she was a millionaire – and a magistrate.

She hadn't warned him she was coming. Hadn't given him a chance to clear up. Skinning-knife in hand, he had watched the top-of-the-range Tesla glide to a stop in front of his game larder, where a couple of open builders' sacks held carcases, offal and, pegged out on boards to dry off, raw pelts with paws and heads still attached, as the Chinese liked them, and heard her high, imperious voice say, 'So it's true. Jago, you sicken me. Unless I'd seen it with my own eyes I would never have believed one of your family could stoop so low. Selling fox skins! Your mother would be horrified and your father must be turning in his grave.'

Shielding his eyes against the low sunlight, he'd attempted excuses – these were urban foxes, vermin. People paid him to get rid of them, he was providing a service – but it was useless. She wouldn't listen. He had always believed she had a soft spot for him but if it had ever existed it was gone now.

'You will leave this house by the end of the week,' her high, hectoring tirade continued, 'and if you make the slightest attempt to claim that I have made you homeless I shall not only report you to the RSPCA but instruct my lawyers to sue you for non-payment of rent, damage to my property, and conducting an unauthorised business involving cruelty to wild animals. Do you understand?'

Before he could even mutter a response, she had turned on her heel and marched back to the car, leaving him shaking with impotent rage.

A week? She must be mad. How could he leave this cottage where he had grown up, secure within its red-brick walls, with the glasshouses in which long-dead gardeners had grown peaches and he had experimented with cannabis plants; with its network of useful sheds and compost heaps which swallowed all manner of refuse and turned it into inoffensive soil? Most bitter of all would be the loss of his game larder, which he had at his own expense equipped with shelves and pulleys, spandrels and hooks for hanging pheasants and pigeons, muntjac deer and hares trapped or snared in the woods.

How was he to find somewhere else to live?

Brooding over this, he had an idea. Would Mr Li agree to let him rent the house where Anne Cutler and young Candy had lived? That would be a poor substitute for The Gardener's Cottage, but a temporary replacement at least. Beggars could not be choosers and besides, if he made himself indispensable to Mr Li, showers of gold might come his way. Nabbing this visitor of Anne Cutler's would be a good start.

Who was he, and what did Mr Li want from him? Politics would be at the bottom of it, no doubt. Wait, watch and listen, thought Jago, and sooner or later he would find out. Knowledge was power, and there were few things Jago enjoyed more than creeping unseen about the woods watching what people were up to when they thought themselves alone.

After a moment he turned the machine and set off on a wide sweep that would take him to The Crooked Scythe from another direction.

Glistening droplets of mist hung between the trees as Candy cantered along the leaf-strewn ride that led from Barleycourt to the big junction of paths known locally as Seven Dials. Any worries she might have had that Fireball would still be stiff after his earlier exertions were soon laid to rest. The sparky chestnut was as full of beans as ever, pretending to shy at an abandoned tractor tyre at the edge of the path, high-blowing in time with his strides, and inclined to jog instead of walk quietly when – following instructions – she came within sight of the rendezvous.

'Approach slowly,' Uncle Will had always insisted, 'and do not speak until I make a signal.'

She calmed Fireball by making him stand, then rein back a couple of paces before letting him walk forward while she scanned the trees ahead for a glimpse of her godfather. Winding through a new plantation of willows, she came on a dark thicket of holly and halted again, wondering if she had misunderstood his directions or overshot the rendezvous.

Then she saw him, standing so close to a tree that he seemed to be part of it, but instead of raising a hand in greeting he let her ride past without making a move to stop her.

Something was wrong. Something was definitely wrong.

Candy's heart gave a painful bump as she realised this was what Uncle Will had often warned her about, and she also remembered what she must do.

'Make no sign that you have seen me and continue on your way. When it is safe I will contact you again,' he'd said.

From the corner of her eye, without turning her head, she registered that every line of him was tense, poised for flight, and guessed that the enemies of whom he had often spoken must have tracked him to this remote patch of woodland. She willed him to melt into the holly thicket in his usual way, but she dared not glance in his direction for fear of giving away his position.

A hundred yards beyond the rendezvous she was beginning to think the danger was past and he had managed his disappearing act when a sudden guttural shout made her swing Fireball round – loud angry voices were followed by a flurry of sickening thumps and a cry of pain. To her horror she saw three burly men in black attacking Uncle William, who was fighting back ferociously as they tried to grab hold of his arms.

'Stop!' she yelled, sending Fireball straight into a canter and driving him into the thick of the melee; she lashed out with all her strength with her whip at the nearest assailant, catching him full across the face. Fireball, who had played polo with his previous owner, was no stranger to rough and tumble; for a moment his charge took the black-clad heavies by surprise and they fell back.

'Let him go!' she screamed, continuing to strike frenziedly at their heads, but a powerful hand twitched the slender whip from her grasp and another seized her lower leg, trying to lift her out of the saddle.

William Yu was gasping, half-throttled by the rope one of his assailants had thrown round his neck, but he saw Candy's danger and managed a hoarse shout: 'Go, child! Tell Pru...'

The rest of the name was cut off as the rope tightened but she got the message. Wheeling Fireball away from the fight, she urged him to a gallop and fled down the track towards Holly Grove. As she reached the crossing of the paths at Seven

Dials, she heard Jago's motorbike coming in from her right and before she could steady him Fireball gave a violent swerve. Candy was catapulted over his shoulder into the overgrown rhododendrons, landing soft but winded among the branches.

When she recovered her breath and stood up, it was to find Jago staring at her. He was holding her pony who was seizing the chance to grab great mouthfuls of grass. 'You OK?' he asked.

She nodded and smiled shakily. 'Thanks for catching him.'

He looked at her intently. 'You were going at such a lick. No wonder you came a cropper.'

Suddenly she remembered why she had been going so fast – Uncle Will...the fight... She said in a rush, 'Jago, something awful has happened. You must help. There's a man being attacked by three thugs. Three against one. They're hurting him. I tried to stop them.'

Maddeningly, he did not move. 'Now, Candy, slow down. What's it all about? Bit of a barney in the woods, eh? What's it got to do with you?'

'Oh, come on,' she pleaded, on the verge of tears. 'If they see two of us, they may let him go.'

'Don't make no sense to me,' he grumbled, but he helped her mount, pulled out the hank of grass tangled round Fireball's bit, and rode the Kawasaki slowly beside her all the way back to the holly thicket.

There was no one in sight. Candy bit her lip, thinking hard. Faint tyre tracks showed her what must have happened: Uncle Will had been forced into a car and carried away. She was too late to save him – worse, she had wasted precious time by falling off and trying to make Jago help. The only thing she could do now was get back to Barleycourt, find Aunt Prue, and tell her the whole story.

Jago was staring about him, the picture of disbelief. He bent to pick up her whip and gave it back to her. 'Here,' he said. 'Satisfied?'

Something in his tone, some buried, unacknowledged pleasure, told her he hadn't wanted her tale to be true. Hadn't wanted to see any evidence of a fight. Had, in fact, deliberately delayed her to give the black-clad thugs the chance to finish their work. How had Jago happened to be here, anyway, at the very moment the fight was taking place? He worked for the Confucius Centre. He was on the side of Uncle Will's enemies. She would never trust him again.

'Yes,' she replied, and turned the pony's head for home.

# CHAPTER SEVEN

HOLDING HER LONG black skirt clear of the ground, Helen stepped through the tent-flap and stopped dead, amazed.

Music and light, heaters working full blast, and fruit and flowers entwined with variegated ivy spiralling up golden pillars had transformed the bare marquee she had helped erect two days ago into a complex of cosy secret grottoes, bars, sitting-out rooms with twinkling lights, and softly carpeted passages leading to the big central dining area, where numbered tables surrounded the dance floor. Along with the annual August Agricultural Show, the triennial Hunt Ball shared with the two adjacent hunts was the year's biggest fund-raiser, and the Committee had spared no expense in making it a glamorous venue.

Jasmine Dymoke, in overall charge of decoration, had persuaded her friends in the local florist to supply tubs of out-of-season flowers and decorative shrubs, together with a whole wall of *sarcococcus confusa* in full bloom, which pervaded the tent with its heady fragrance. Harvey Joliffe, who often acted as the amateur whipper-in, and whose father was a wine merchant, had supplied champagne and spirits, while the Chairman of one adjacent hunt committee came good with both red and white wine. Two steps up on a dais, resplendent in white silk shirts with gold-frogged waistcoats, the live band were playing themselves in quietly as a background to the excited chatter and popping of corks as revellers found their tables: two impressive speakers either side of their platform hinted at deafening decibels to come.

'We're Table 18, Isabel's party,' said Jonah, at Helen's shoulder, urging her forward. 'Come on. I'll show you the way.'

It seemed very odd to be following his spare, limping figure instead of having tall Noel by her side, and for a moment she was tempted to run back to the car. Jonah must have sensed this, because he turned and took her hand with a smile.

'You can do this,' he murmured. 'It'll be all right. We'll both be all right.'

In the well-cut scarlet tailcoat with pale yellow facings that had belonged to his father, with starched dress shirt under a cream waistcoat, shining Hunt buttons, snowy breeches, and patent leather pumps, he was as well got-up as any man there, but he would never have Noel's effortless presence and charisma. Nevertheless, with his warm hand gripping hers as friends clustered round, Helen felt her momentary panic recede. He was right. She *could* do this: chatter and laugh, eat, drink and possibly even dance without letting anyone see the emptiness she felt inside.

'Well done, darling,' said her father, close behind. 'Now you're over the worst. The rest will be easy.'

Isabel greeted her with a piercing shriek. '*Sweetie!* You made it. I'm so glad. I've a thousand things to ask you. Come and sit with me, Mr Robb...'

'Martin, please.'

'OK then, Martin.' She patted the chair beside her, lowered her voice and said confidentially, 'As you probably know I'm a magistrate, and we're all just longing to know how the police are getting on with their enquiry. None of us has heard a word.'

'I wish I could tell you,' said Robb, 'but they're playing their cards pretty close to their chests. No arrests imminent, I gather, but they're exploring every avenue.'

'And you're sticking to the script.'

Robb chuckled. 'Very boring of me, I know. Tell me, do you have a slap-up party like this every year?'

'Lord, no! It would ruin us. Once every three years is our ration, taking turns with the adjacent Hunts. Of course, each of us tries to put on the best show...'

She embarked on a detailed explanation of Hunt finances and strategies and Helen relaxed, glad the heat had been deflected for the time being at least.

Ricky Owen, escorting a pretty blonde off the polished floor, sketched a little bow and asked her to dance. By the time she returned to her table, her plate of smoked salmon had been replaced with a good-looking slice of beef Wellington, Isabel had switched her attention to Jonah, and her father – with an expression on his face she knew well – was listening intently to Prue, who had ruthlessly swapped seats with Dora Marshall to be next to him and was talking fast and low.

'I need your advice, Martin,' she said urgently. 'I honestly don't know what to do.'

'What's it about?'

'Well, you know my niece, Candy? She came to me yesterday almost in hysterics, plastered in mud, having fallen off her pony, and told me an extraordinary story. I – I don't know whether to believe it or not, but I can't just ignore it.'

'Go on.'

'She says that ever since Anne was killed, she has been meeting a man she calls her godfather. He used to visit Anne in that cottage you helped me clear out. He texts Candy to tell her where to meet him when she goes out riding alone, sometimes once a week, sometimes once a fortnight, always in great secrecy because he says his enemies are trying to track him down.'

Robb stirred. 'What does he look like, this godfather?'

'She says he's Chinese.'

'Ah. What's he called?'

Prue leaned closer, talking fast. 'She clammed up completely when I asked his name. Said Anne had forbidden her to mention it because it was dangerous for him. I hate bullying her, but I had to be quite fierce, and say I couldn't do anything to help unless she told me.' She shook her head. 'She can be pretty obstinate, you know. Just like Anne, but after a long stand-off, she saw sense. It's William. William Yu. She calls him Uncle Will.'

It rang a bell with Robb: a loud and specific bell. 'The Hong Kong dissident? The chap who writes those *Blast Off* pieces in *Scene from the East*?'

'That's the one. I know various people on the staff, so I got through to his editor, who was extremely cagey but admitted she was worried that she couldn't contact him. Apparently he has been roughed up several times by Chinese – ahem – security guards outside their Embassy where he was leading demos. Now he seems to have disappeared.'

'Your niece says she saw him fighting off three men in the woods? Has she any evidence?'

'Not really. She went back with Jago Smith, who just happened to be passing...'

'Hmm. Interesting.'

'But there was nothing to see. Nobody there. Jago picked up her whip which was lying on the ground...'

'Wait a bit. Did she know how she'd lost it?'

'She said one of the thugs grabbed it. She was using it to beat them.'

'Well, that's evidence of a kind.' Rob thought for a moment, then said, ' Look, I'm sorry to abandon you but I must go and do some telephoning, right away. Keep all this to yourself, and oh, make my excuses to our hostess, right?'

She nodded; and he walked decisively to the back of the tent, detoured past the Gents and out into the dark night.

*****

Dinner finished, noise levels rose and the tables began to fragment as people moved to sit with other friends or dance. Furthest from the music, the Old and Bold settled in for sessions of gossip and steady drinking; youngsters retreated to throw shapes in the dimly lit disco, and the few really accomplished dancers swooped and glided across the floor in classic waltzes and foxtrots.

As usual, the amateur horn-blowing contest produced some excruciating parps and squawks, each scarlet-faced competitor greeted with ribald comments and groans; and a great cheer went up when Fergal the pro, exasperated by their ineptitude, strolled to the dais and, taking his own battered horn from his pocket, showed them how it should be done.

'Auction next,' said Isabel. 'That's always fun. Where's your father? He'll enjoy this.'

Helen hadn't seen him leave. She had danced a couple of times and stoically listened to Isabel's monologue about her plans for next summer's campaign to win international dressage competitions, and how Suleiman the Magnificent would wipe the floor with all his rivals. Unsurprisingly she included a good many refinements to his current care and training which were going to mean extra work for Helen's staff.

'I'm really pleased with the way he's come on since I moved him to Barleycourt,' she said winningly. 'You look after him beautifully, but...' Helen had expected the 'but' – 'now's the time to give him just a little more oomph, to put an edge on his performance. I've heard of this marvellous stuff that you put in his feed every other day. Ruinously expensive, of course, but all the real stars swear by it...'

And perhaps they have shares in the company that makes this magic potion, thought Helen. Perhaps they spend more time actually schooling their dressage stars instead of bragging about their potential. Where, oh where was Jonah, who usually deflected this repetitive avalanche of tosh away from her, and could talk Isabel down from her crazy dreams of international glory? He had left their table to confer with fellow bigwigs on the Hunt Committee, and now she saw him rise and limp up the steps on to the dais.

'Oh, look! They've persuaded Jonah to be auctioneer,' said Isabel. 'That's brave of him. It's usually done by No...'

By Noel.

Too late Isabel remembered to whom she was talking, and put her hand to her mouth.

Tears stung Helen's eyes. She rose with a muttered excuse, and stumbled through the tables to the back of the marquee. She couldn't watch this or listen to the jokes and noisy banter as Jonah ran the bidding up. She had done her bit by coming to the Ball. No one would notice if she left.

After the warmth and noise inside the marquee, the park was cold, quiet, and very dark, but the light on her iPhone was enough to pick out the rows of cars parked beside the track, with the cattle grid and stable yard beyond. Mercifully dry underfoot, too, so her flimsy shoes coped well enough with its rough surface, but though the tears had dried on her cheeks, her ballgown left one shoulder bare and despite her velvet cloak she was shivering by the time she reached the yard.

There was a set of electric rails for drying horse clothing in the tack room, and although Jeremy took care that the little wood-burning stove was extinguished at night, there would still be some residual heat. Candy had volunteered to babysit Angus that night but she was a light sleeper and was bound to be curious that Helen had come home so early.

Easier to avoid unwelcome questions: without switching on the yard lights, she used her phone to unlock the tack room and slipped inside. With both hands flat on the still-warm top of the stove, she allowed herself to cry, raging inside against the cruel fate that had snatched Noel from her.

A gossamer touch against her legs, a tiny mew and she bent to stroke the stable cat, who had moved her surviving kittens into this cosy haven.

'Sorry, Kitty. Not breakfast time yet,' she sniffed, wiping her eyes and kneeling down to shine her phone into their box. One ginger, one black with a white shirt-front: at three weeks old, they were irresistible, with wide open eyes and short fluffy tails. Helen scooped them both up to cuddle, and was holding them under her chin when she heard a scuffling noise she couldn't identify.

Rats? One of the horses moving round his box, getting up or lying down?

Carefully replacing the kittens in their box, she moved to the door and stood listening. A moment's silence, then the noise again and this time she realised it was coming from the stallion's stable, a spacious double loose box, so divided by a barrier of sheeted hurdles that two thirds were given over to Suleiman and the remainder allocated to Sarah, his donkey 'nannie'. A feeding passage ran behind this double stable, and a long manger. When Sarah had finished her few pony cubes she would try to reach the stallion's large and delicious feed on his side of the manger. Could that account for the scuffling?

A more dangerous possibility occurred to her: the stallion might be rolling in his stable. This could result in a twisted gut, at worst, or becoming 'cast' – stuck with hoofs against the wall, unable to lever himself away. She had seen this happen with dire results.

No. A grunt that was definitely human in origin scotched that explanation. More scuffling, another grunt and a curse. With a chill that went to the marrow of her bones, Helen realised there was an intruder in the stallion's box.

All her security fears flooded back. Since Suleiman's previous escapade, the half-door of his box, which opened on to the yard, had been locked at night with a 4-digit combination which took a few seconds to open. The main light-switch was just inside the door. The feeding passage offered more direct access, so dropping her hampering cloak, she left the warmth of the tack room, dashed along the covered walkway and shone her phone into the stallion's stable, dreading what she might see.

Suleiman was not rolling, but standing backed into a corner, head up, wild-eyed, though in the narrow beam of light at first it was difficult to know what was wrong. He was stamping and swinging his hindquarters from side to side as if rubbing his tail against the wall, while leaning over from the other side of the barrier the donkey's head craned down at something dark among the pale wood-shavings, close beneath Suleiman's hind legs.

A long roll of...what? It looked like a heavy log.

She focused the beam on it and it stirred, both hands clamped to its middle as it tried to wriggle away from those threatening hoofs.

'Help!' it groaned.

She was tempted to leave it where it was while she sought assistance. It would take five minutes at least to run back to the marquee where Johnny and Jeremy would probably be in the bar with Seamus, and Jonah still conducting the auction. Who else? Isabel? Likely to make things worse. The safety of Suleiman must be her top priority, and in five minutes who knew what damage the intruder might do to him?

'Don't move,' she ordered, and ran to the feed shed for a scoop of the stallion's favourite coarse mix. Keying in the combination as fast as her shaking fingers would allow, she opened the half-door and switched on the light.

'Here, boy. Something nice,' she told the horse, tipping it into the manger. The donkey gave a muted bray: 'Me, too.'

The black bundle on the stable floor didn't move.

Suleiman did not want to leave his captive. He suspected a trick. Only when Helen picked up a handful of the feed and dropped it in the donkey's side of the trough for her to plunge her nose in did the stallion come forward reluctantly to start eating his own ration. As he moved, Helen saw a loaded syringe lying in the shavings where he had been standing, and bent to pick it up.

Behind her a sudden flurry of movement caught her by surprise. She had barely time to straighten up before a stunning blow to the back of her head sent her reeling towards the door, seeing stars. Suleiman whipped round, snorting. Half blinded, Helen staggered outside, aware of the dark shadow following her through, and just managed to slam the door shut before a second blow knocked her out cold.

# CHAPTER EIGHT

'WAKE UP, HELS. Time to wake up,' said Noel's voice as Helen tried to open her eyes. Had she slept through the alarm? She was cold, and ached all over. Where was she?

Memory filtered back, first in a trickle, then a rush. It wasn't Noel's voice but his brother's – the unmistakable family voice. Not the alarm because it was still night, and the hard bed she was lying on was not her own but a heap of horse rugs in – the smell she had always loved made this plain – the tack room. The anxious faces looking down at her belonged to Jonah and to Jasmine Dymoke, dressed to kill, wanting to know how she had come to be lying, unconscious, outside the stallion's box in her ball-going finery.

'Someone hit me,' she mumbled.

'What?' exclaimed Jonah.

'Say that again, poppet.'

She tried to sit up but her head span and she sank back on the heap of rugs, becoming aware of buckles and straps digging into her back. Aware, too, of the prime cause of the trouble.

'Suleiman! Is he OK?'

They exchanged a glance. 'Now relax, poppet,' said Jasmine firmly. 'He's quite OK. There's nothing to worry about.'

Now Helen's voice had come back. She said jerkily, 'There was someone in his box. Must have climbed the half-door. He had a syringe. Sully got him pinned in a corner.' She stopped, exhausted.

'Did he kick him?' Jasmine's face was alight with excitement.

'Squashed him against the wall, I think. He was lying down and I thought he might be dead, but when I opened the door he dashed out.'

'Hitting you on the way,' said Jonah grimly. 'Right. Johnny and Jeremy will be here any moment, and we'll all check round the yard and see there are no other uninvited guests. Will you stay here with Hels, Jasmine?'

'Sure.'

Helen's head ached, and she closed her eyes. There was silence for a while after the men went out, then faintly on the breeze came the strains of the *Post-Horn Gallop*, bringing memories of other Hunt Balls, other places, other times when Noel had been at her side. Tears ran down her cheeks.

'Wake up, poppet,' said Jasmine. 'Don't drift away again. I'll see if there's an aspirin in my bag.'

# CHAPTER NINE

'THAT SHOULD COVER you from all angles.' The chief superintendent signed the search warrant with his indecipherable scrawl and handed it to Robb. He leaned back in his chair. 'It will cause a diplomatic stink, no doubt, but I only wish I could go with you. I've been wanting an excuse to take a look inside that outfit for quite a while. All that rubbish about culture! Nothing but a nest of spies, if you ask me, which our government is fool enough to tolerate.' He sighed gustily. 'Well, I must get on. Nice meeting you, and let me know what happens. Good hunting!'

'Thank you, sir.'

Robb hurried down the steps and found Sergeant Winter waiting in the police station car park, chatting to two other drivers. His intense telephoning session last night had borne fruit: Jim Winter, his long-time deputy, had dropped everything – 'nothing that can't wait, sir...' and arrived at Barleycourt at two in the morning, to be briefed over breakfast.

'Bacon and two eggs, Jim?' offered Robb, who knew his Sergeant's appetite. Jim Winter was a lean, muscular young man who had helped Robb out of many a tight spot, though his ultra-correct attitude sometimes clashed with his boss's more liberal interpretation of the law. He was always hungry, could eat for four and never put on an ounce, but their interests were poles apart. Winter spent his leave mountain-biking and deep-sea diving, and relaxed with martial arts and computer games. He was secretly in love with Sally, Robb's middle daughter.

As he wolfed down one laden slice of toast after another, Robb filled him in with the background to their raid.

'They're a territorial lot, and may not be glad to see us,' he added. 'We know they've got at least three heavies.'

Winter grinned. 'Sounds right up my street. Have you spoken to the RSPCA? They might want to be involved.'

Robb nodded. 'They're happy to leave it to us. I checked yesterday that it's an offence, all right.'

'Oh, yes. That's a clear contravention of the Wildlife Act,' the RSPCA inspector had confirmed. 'Anyone trying to export skins would need a licence. Fur farming is illegal in this country, as you know, and anyway foxes have never been legally classified as vermin. They are wild animals. Anyone guilty of maltreating them or killing them by poisoning, gassing, or asphyxiating is liable for a £5,000 fine.'

'That's just what I wanted to know,' said Robb, thinking that Mr Li had more than one question to answer.

'Can I come with you?' asked Prue, businesslike in a well-cut rust-coloured trouser suit and sensible brogues. 'Oh, please! I've always longed to take part in a police raid – *Go, go, go!* and bashing down locked doors. After all, my sister worked for the Centre. I could say she left things in her desk.'

'I'm afraid not,' said Robb. Searching the buildings would be enough of a circus without helpful interventions by outsiders. 'I'm not planning to do any door-bashing,' he added. 'Just a polite request to have a look round.'

*****

The polite request was immediately refused by the shaven-headed gatekeeper, who looked suspiciously at the small convoy of yellow-chequered cars and reached for his smartphone. Standing just behind Robb, Winter did the same.

'You waiting here,' said the gatekeeper, after a brief guttural exchange. Robb looked at him closely. Had that mark across his face been made by Candy's whip?

'Please open the gate. I have business with Mr Li.'

Another glare. Another short conversation, and the gate slowly swung inward. Winter drove through, followed by the other cars, and parked across the front door.

Ever-smiling Mr Li greeted Robb with no outward sign of worry, though he looked askance at the uniformed police escort. 'To what do I owe this pleasure?' he asked.

Robb gave his name and showed the search warrant. 'Mr Li, I have reason to believe that you have been trading in fox skins without a licence which is against the law, being contrary to the provisions of the Wildlife and Countryside Act. I therefore wish to search these premises.'

'To search for fox skins!' Mr Li displayed bewildered innocence. 'You say it is forbidden to kill foxes? But many people hunt foxes for pleasure and sometimes they are killed.'

No time to explain the ins and outs of the Hunting Act on the doorstep while no doubt Mr Li's minions were busily clearing away all evidence of illegal activity.

Robb said to Winter, 'Go ahead. I'll deal with this,' and watched the team spread out in a well trained pack to examine the contents of the sheds and outhouses, kennels and stables of Dene Manor.

'Use your noses, lads,' he'd briefed them. 'Untanned skins smell pretty bad, so they're unlikely to keep them in the house. If you catch a whiff of something nasty, follow it up.'

The searchers worked methodically, opening doors, examining the contents of boxes and sacks, climbing into lofts and using stepladders to reach high shelves. They found a large quantity of surveillance equipment and electronic material, but no skins.

'This is an outrage. My Embassy shall hear of it. There will be consequences,' warned Mr Li.

Robb did not reply. He continued to watch the searchers, standing at Li's side to prevent him signalling to the other Chinese who clustered on the doorstep, talking and gesticulating. Winter was standing in shadow, keeping his eyes on the gatekeeper, who had retreated to his lodge and disappeared inside.

Presently a door at the back opened and shut quietly. Padding down the lodge path at a surprising speed for one of his bulk, Shaven-head disappeared round the corner of the old walled garden. Winter followed and was just in time to see him press the button of a roll-over garage door and hurry inside.

Winter sprinted to duck under the door before it closed. The interior was brightly lit by long fluorescent tubes which revealed two big HiLux trucks parked side by side, and two electric Tesla saloons. Against the back wall was a cubbyhole full of mechanical gear. Moving swiftly at a bow-legged run, Shaven-head had gone straight past the cars to the back of the garage and seemed to be tussling with a padlock.

Winter's quick glance took in the figure slumped in a chair that was chained to a metal stanchion before Shaven-head looked round and saw him. Instantly he launched a furious attack, catching Winter with a punch to the head that could have shattered his skull had he not rocked sideways, deflecting the force of the blow. Even so, his neck cracked almost to his shoulder and stars exploded behind his eyes.

Bending swiftly, he caught the gatekeeper's right leg and up-ended him, then with a strong effort flipped him on to his stomach and knelt on him, wrenching his bent left arm painfully upward behind his shoulder blade. Shaven-head grunted and used his powerful stomach muscles to try to throw him off, kicking both legs and squirming so violently that for an instant Winter wondered if he had bitten off more than he could chew.

He wrenched the captive arm higher and said loudly in his ear, 'Where are the skins?' but even if the gatekeeper understood he didn't intend to answer. He continued to struggle, thrashing and kicking, while Winter pinned him down.

Impasse. Unable to get at Google *Translate* in his pocket, he had no means to communicate and, as well as being several stone heavier, Shaven-head was extremely strong. Without control of his opponent's free arm, Winter's handcuffs were useless: his head was singing from that first punch and it was becoming a question of who would hold out longest.

From outside came faintly the shouts of police searchers, but they might have been on the moon for all the help they could give him. Another heave, another squirm, and he felt his grip broken, left holding nothing but the loose blue tunic the gatekeeper wore. Winter was lifted bodily, as if from a bucking horse, and a savage chop from the edge of Shaven-head's hand numbed his shoulder. His collarbone snapped audibly. Oh no, he thought as pain shot up his arm. Not again!

A one-armed opponent was no match for Shaven-head, and now it was Winter's turn to lie prone, protecting his head as best he could, while blows rained down on him. Winter played stunned, aware that Shaven-head had scrambled up to press a switch by the nearest car. A section of floor slid back,

— Death of a Dealer —

revealing an inspection pit beneath, and a nauseating smell of decaying flesh wafted out and made him gag.

Fox pelts, he thought. A moment later it was clear that skins were not the only things to be hidden there. The bound and gagged prisoner was flung in bodily and Winter knew with cold horror that he would be next. Raising himself painfully on to all fours, he crawled underneath a parked HiLux and lay flat, gripping part of the steering to stop the gatekeeper dragging him out. He felt the man's hand groping for his legs, but drew them up to his chest and out of harm's way. Shaven-head's bulk made it impossible for him to get under the car, but he had another card to play.

Winter heard him pad away to the back of the garage, and a moment later the jingle of keys and a sharp click told him the vehicle had been unlocked. Then the engine started with a roar, and the car began to move.

*****

The searchers had drawn a blank. They gathered round Robb for instructions, disappointed and panting.

The corners of the sergeant's mouth tightened. 'Zero.'

Did Mr Li's smile widen a fraction? 'There will be consequences,' he repeated. 'This is an outrage.'

Robb didn't answer. He was counting heads. 'Where's Winter?' he said sharply.

An observant young constable spoke up. 'Saw him following that fellow from the gatehouse, couple of minutes back.' He pointed.

An ugly customer and twice Winter's size: Robb's skin prickled. 'After him,' he snapped. 'Quick as you like.'

*****

As the HiLux jerked forward, Winter let go of the steering and scrambled clear of the wheels, ignoring the sickening grating of his collarbone. In his haste to leave the driver's seat to nail his victim, Shaven-head let the vehicle shunt into the car in front, and both of them crashed into the back wall. As the clang of metal died away, there was a shout from outside.

'Police. Open the door!' followed two seconds later by the thud of the battering ram.

*Thump. Thump. Thump-thump!*

The roll-up's lock gave way and the police searchers poured into the garage, with horrified gasps as they inhaled the foul stench. Shaven-head backed away, his hands high.

'Cuff him,' said the sergeant. 'Now, what have we got here?' He peered into the inspection pit.

'William Yu, at a guess,' said Robb, who had followed them and was trying to breathe as shallowly as possible. 'Poor fellow, he looks in a bad way. Let's get him out of here and away from these stinking skins.'

Winter had hauled himself painfully to his feet and was checking his injuries. Bruises a-plenty and a fast-closing eye, and of course the broken collarbone. He thought on the whole that he had escaped lightly.

'Spoilt your beauty for you, has he?' said Robb heartlessly.

'Nothing that won't mend, sir.'

With William Yu, inert but still breathing, carried to the police van on a collapsible stretcher, and the rolled-up, salted fox-skins carried in garden sacks by two disgusted constables, Robb made his way to where Li was still rooted to the spot. His smile had become a grimace.

'Mr Li, I am arresting you on a charge of kidnap and false imprisonment,' said Robb formally. 'Also of cruelty to animals and illegally trading in wild animal skins without a licence. You do not have to say anything, but anything you do say may be used in evidence against you...'

# CHAPTER TEN

'TAKE A LOOK at these.' Jonah put a small basket on Helen's desk and watched her examine the contents.

A scalpel, two loaded syringes, a phial of antibiotic and another of painkiller, a pack of surgical gloves, a twitch, hobbles, a head-torch... She looked at him in bewilderment.

'Where did you find these?'

'Johnny found them in Suleiman's box. Mixed in with the shavings, scattered all over the place. He thinks – and I agree – that your midnight intruder planned to geld him.'

'But – but who –?' she stuttered, too appalled to think straight. Castrating the stallion would remove much of his value, depriving him of his pride and presence, and to perform such an operation in a stable in near-darkness might lead to serious infection at least, if it did not kill him. She was filled with impotent rage against the pain humans inflict on animals, particularly horses.

Jonah was watching her reaction. 'Horrible, isn't it?'

'Sickening.'

'Someone really hates Isabel,' he mused. 'I can think *who* might try this, and you probably can too, but I can't for the life of me think *why*.' He fiddled with the papers on her desk, picking them up and putting them down in the wrong order, but she resisted the temptation to snap at him. 'Nor can I think how to prove it. We'll have to get your Dad on to this. Where is he?'

'Stopping Gus falling off Seamus' tractor,' she said with a half-smile. It was a blessed relief when she could concentrate on her accounts without the little boy round her feet. 'Are you going to tell Izzy about these?' She pointed at the basket's contents.

'Not till I've something more than suspicion to go on.'

'But we can't keep her horse here any longer! Not after this. It's too dangerous, Jonah. He's too valuable, and too easy to get at. I shan't have a moment's peace until he leaves the yard for good.'

'Now calm down, Hels,' he said as if she was an over-excited filly. 'You've had a nasty shock but it's not going to happen again, I'll see to that. As of today, I'm having CCTV and an alarm put in Suleiman's stable, and I wish I'd done it before this happened. That horse is going to be guarded 24/7 and as safe as Fort Knox. He'll be much better off with us than he would be with anyone else.'

'We – ell...' She was only partly reassured.

'So stop worrying, OK?'

'I'll try.'

'That's the spirit. Oh, and when your Dad comes in, tell him I'd like a word.'

*****

Christmas was upon them, and with it a spell of mild, soft weather, temperatures in double digits at mid afternoon, and reckless snowdrops already inches above the ground, but no one at Barleycourt felt much like celebrating. Gus was too young and Candy subdued and silent, too preoccupied with the loss of her mother to enjoy traditional stockings and flaming puddings. Time and again, Helen thought she was squaring up to say something – to ask some important question – but on each occasion the moment passed and she said nothing.

As usual the irrepressible Jasmine brought a sack of apples and carrots for all the horses in the yard, and the stable staff were presented with Christmas bonuses, but in other respects the day passed quietly in the same routine as ever – feeding, grooming, mucking-out – with a flurry of activity as darkness fell and everyone with a horse to ride prepared for the Boxing Day Meet.

'I want any horse that isn't hunting turned out in a New Zealand rug tomorrow,' said Jonah, visiting the tack room for the usual briefing. 'It'll do them good to get a bite of grass and whatever sun there is on their backs.'

'What about Suleiman?' asked Helen who had been checking his stable compulsively in the week since the Hunt Ball, despite the new locks and CCTV.

'He and his donkey can go out in the Lime Paddock. It's very sheltered and frankly I'd feel happier to know he was outside rather than trapped in a small space when we're all out. Jeremy and Johnny will be driving the lorries, and Seamus has volunteered to take the low-loader to Elliotts' yard for more straw. The last thing we want is to run short of bedding over the New Year.'

He looked around. 'All right, everyone? Any questions? Oh, and Hels, before you ask, I shall be taking young Gus in my Land Rover. He'll enjoy that. I've put the child-seat in it already.'

This was off-script. Startled, she stared at him. She had been planning to use the little boy as an excuse not to go. 'Oh, but...'

'So you will be free to ride Lucky Dip.'

She had always found the Boxing Day Meet an ordeal. Too crowded, too noisy, too jolly. Under the shadow of the grim, cannon-ball scarred walls of Seizan Castle, it was held in the town square where every hostelry dispensed lavish drinks, crisps and sausages to a jostling mass of all ages, who shouted and squealed and encouraged any hounds that escaped from the range of the whipper-in's thong to put muddy paws on their shoulders and lick their faces, to submit to the patting and petting of children, to gobble things that would upset their digestions, to chase cats and small dogs and generally misbehave.

Fergal the huntsman always said that the Boxing Day Meet gave him grey hairs, though he played his starring role to perfection, smiling and accepting thimblefuls of port – which usually ended up trickling into his horse's mane – and answering ill-informed questions with polite patience, while Harvey rated and cursed would-be absconders under his breath.

There were also far too many once-a-year riders and track-suited foot-soldiers for hounds to follow a line, and a bunch of banner-waving sabs, screaming obscenities and spraying aerosols to distract any hound that wandered too near them would complete the picture.

Jonah held her gaze, amused and slightly challenging. He knew she didn't want to go and was pulling the rug from under her. She wouldn't give him the satisfaction of knowing the strategy had worked – not in front of her livery clients.

'OK,' she said unwillingly. 'If you really think it's safe to leave the yard empty all day.'

'Safe as houses. Of course it is. And it won't be all day – more like four hours or so.'

'Well – thanks for offering to take Gus off my hands. Very good of you,' she said coolly, and he smiled.

'It'll be a pleasure for both of us.'

It wasn't until he left the tack room that she realised he had not mentioned what her father would be doing next day. Probably teaming up with Jabez Crump again, she thought. I'll ask him at supper.

But supper brought a text from Robb to tell her he had been called away on official business, and hoped to return the following evening. Mopping up after the raid on the Confucius Centre, she thought, and looked forward to hearing all about it.

\*\*\*\*\*

'You goin' to the Meet tomorrow?' asked Jago, appearing with his motorbike as Candy brought her pony in from the field.

'Yes,' she said shortly, making it clear she was busy; didn't want to talk, particularly to Jago. She hadn't forgotten his behaviour when her godfather was in peril.

'Don't be like that, Candy,' he wheedled. 'I thought you and me was friends. Look, I brought you a Christmas present.'

Reluctantly she took the small box and opened it. Inside was a little golden chain necklace with the letter C suspended as a pendant.

'Thank you.' She didn't know how to tell him she didn't want necklaces from him, now or ever.

'I know it's only cheap, but it's pretty,' he went on, playing for sympathy. 'I'd give you a real gold one if I could, but now they're closing down the Centre I've lost my home and my job…'

She didn't answer. She had no wish to listen to him whingeing about how poor he was and how badly the Chinese had treated him. Silently she led Fireball through the gate and turned towards the stable yard.

Jago followed. 'Aren't you going to give me a kiss, then? For the necklace?'

Silence. Since the answer was evidently no, he changed tack. 'So you're takin' this fellow hunting tomorrow, are you? Want a hand to clean him up?'

Candy said clearly, so there should be no confusion. 'We're all hunting tomorrow. Everyone. Any horse that isn't hunting will be turned out in a rug.'

'What about Mrs Murray's dad? The copper?'

'He's had to go back to London. And now, please stop asking me questions. I've got a lot to do, even if you haven't.'

'Have it your own way,' he grumbled. 'There's no pleasing some girls.'

*****

Very occasionally, the complicated operation that is a hunting morning in a livery stable goes like clockwork. Riders turn up in good time with all their kit, no last-minute panics over missing gloves or whips; horses clatter without hesitation up the ramp and range themselves sideways into the lorry's partitions; engines start sweetly without choking and spluttering, and everyone agrees on the best route to the Meet and where to leave the horsebox.

On Boxing Day the sun shone, the puddles were barely skimmed with ice, the very air smelled of spring.

'I wish it was always like this,' sighed Jasmine, herself deliciously redolent of aromatherapy shower gel.

'Can't last,' said Ricky, who tended to look on the dark side.

Helen spent the short journey checking and rechecking that she had done everything she could to keep the stable yard safe in their absence. She was still uneasy about leaving it unguarded, and would have liked to know that her father was there to keep an eye on things.

Suleiman had signalled his pleasure in being turned out by giving some spectacular bucks and high-stepping extempore *piaffes* and *levades* before joining the donkey in her steady grazing. Helen watched until she was sure they had settled and the gate was securely locked before she turned away.

Long before they reached the town square, a stream of lorries and trailers was clogging the narrow streets, and it seemed as if all the world and his wife had come out to see hounds.

'Good job we started early,' said Ricky, as they swung into a side street and under the arch of the old coaching inn.

Down the ramp clattered the five horses, and Helen surveyed them critically. Although they were all experienced travellers, Ricky's big bay Democrat had sweated up as usual; Candy's pony Fireball had lost his tail bandage; her own black mare Lucky Dip had managed to pull her bridle over one ear, which gave her a curiously raffish appearance, and Daisy, the plain-headed, reliable grey cob she had lent to Isabel, was still sporting yellow stable stains which should have been washed off. Only the neat, sweet, chestnut thoroughbred Betsinda really passed muster but then, thought Helen, the Boxing Day Meet was no beauty contest. Everyone was out to support the Hunt and enjoy themselves – so why was she dreading the next hours and already longing to go home?

'Wake up, Hels,' said Jonah, appearing at her elbow. 'They're unboxing hounds in the Castle courtyard. You'd better get a move on.'

They all mounted hastily and rode into the middle of the town square where a wave of cheers and clapping greeted the appearance of Fergal and his hounds, flanked by two of the four Joint-Masters, with Harvey the whipper-in just behind.

Fergal wheeled the pack neatly into the angle of two walls, from which Harvey's whip, supported by those of both kennelmen, dared them to stray. A forest of smartphones captured every move as they sat and scratched, or raised questing noses towards the burger van and gave the occasional muted yowl.

On the far side of the square, Corky O'Sullivan, easily recognisable in cargo shorts and long black ponytail, was inciting a posse of sabs to shout and wave placards saying STOP HUNTING! but there seemed to be fewer than usual and their words were lost in the general good-natured hubbub.

Fireball was becoming agitated, dancing on the spot and bunching his hindquarters as the crowd pressed close to him. 'What shall I do?' said Candy anxiously. 'I'm afraid he'll kick someone.'

'Stay near me. Talk to him,' said Helen. 'We'll go where it's quieter – on the other side of the square.'

They worked their way through the jostling press of bodies, with Fireball's nose almost buried in Lucky Dip's tail, until they reached the relative calm of the steps to the Town Hall on the far side of the square. From this vantage point they could watch how people clustered most tightly round the trays of drinks being carried in and out of pubs, and how they continually edged closer to the centre of attention where the Hunt servants were still keeping the hounds in disciplined formation despite all attempts to distract them.

'Look, there's Jonah,' said Candy, pointing across the square.

And just what has he done with my son? thought Helen, but a moment later she saw that care of Gus had for the moment been delegated to Dora Marshall, who was carrying the little boy on one hip while holding an ice-cream cornet for him to lick. Even at this distance, his mother could see that he looked grubby, sticky, and supremely happy.

For twenty minutes or so they watched and waited. Fireball ceased his fidgeting and stood calmly while Candy fiddled with her saddlery, first shortening her stirrup leathers a couple of holes, then letting them down again. It was clear she had something on her mind.

'Hels,' she said at last in such a quiet, constrained murmur that Helen had to bend down from her saddle to hear, 'did you know that... that William – *oh!*' she broke off as a short toot of the horn warned that Fergal thought it time to move.

'That William what?' prompted Helen, but the moment for confidences was gone.

'I'll tell you later.'

In a clatter of hoofs that echoed around the square, and sped on their way by an accompanying cheer from the bystanders, the Hunt surged out of the town square and set off across the Castle Meadow.

Traditionally the first covert to be drawn was barely a hundred yards along the road and steeply uphill to the rough parkland behind the Castle.

'Stick close to me,' Helen advised. 'There's always a bit of a scrimmage until the Field sorts itself out. We'll stay at the back and catch up once they're over the first fence. My guess is that they'll pick up the scent in that spinney at the top of the hill.'

The few remnants of the Scots pines allegedly planted as a gesture of support for Jacobites and known locally as the 'Charlie Trees' had long ago been overwhelmed by brambles and scrub, and into this prickly haven the pack plunged eagerly.

Marjorie Whittle, once again Acting Field Master, held back the cavalcade well below the summit to give hounds a chance to find. A cloud of steam rose from the horses, and several of the sporting mothers leading their children on Shetland ponies discovered just how hard it was to keep up with a four-legged animal, no matter how small and shaggy.

'I'm cooked,' groaned one, pressing her hand to her ribs. 'No, darling, I can't go any faster.'

'Bellows to mend,' observed Ricky with a grin.

He and other regulars subscribers had a fair idea of where today's hunt would end up; the question was which of three possible routes would it take to get there? The most direct involved jumping some seriously hairy obstacles, hardly suitable for such a mixed Field; the second would mean a lot of roadwork on the narrow web of lanes behind the castle; the third would delight the huntsman because it crossed the extensive swampy ground from which many a real live fox launched his raids on local hen-houses.

For five minutes they waited with mounting impatience, listening to the occasional whimper as hounds appeared and disappeared among the clumps of brambles. Pheasants rose noisily over the spinney and planed away downwind, and there was a short burst of high, excited yipping as a very small deer made a hurried break from covert pursued by two hounds who should have known better.

'Look, Mummy! There's a fox!' cried a child.

'Muntjac,' chorused the better-informed.

'Ware haunch!'

Harvey's whip cracked, and casting him guilty looks, the culprits returned to working through the brambles.

The Field was growing restive.

'I said there wouldn't be any scent today. It's too warm,' complained Isabel Garraway, but hardly had she spoken before a spine-tingling outburst of hound music brought the whole pack leaping and bounding out of the spinney and down the steep slope on the far side of the park. Beyond it lay the marsh, with puddles sparkling in the winter sun.

'Now we're off,' said Jasmine with satisfaction.

'*Teroot-teroot*, Gone away,' went Fergal's horn, as he and Patrick, his chestnut Irish Sport Horse, took the shortest way downhill at a breakneck gallop, while more cautious souls began a careful zigzag.

'Stick to me,' said Helen. 'There'll be a bottleneck at the bottom but we'll avoid it.'

Sure enough, a dozen horses were queuing to jump the tiger trap in the park boundary when they arrived on flatter ground. Helen made instead for the cattle grid and swiftly opened the narrow gate beside it. She and Candy crammed through before anyone else noticed this alternative route, and crossed the minor road beyond. Fergal's red coat was already two fields away, on the edge of the marsh, and hounds were fanned out in a broad swathe, puzzling out the line.

Fireball was pulling hard and Candy, scarlet in the face, set her left hand's knuckles against his neck and tugged unavailingly on the other rein. 'I can't stop him,' she gasped.

'Don't fight him. Let him have his head,' advised Helen. 'He won't go far without me.'

Sure enough, once his nose was in front of Lucky Dip's, Fireball's pace slackened and, followed by everyone who had negotiated the tiger trap they trotted along the narrow road towards the gate leading to the marsh. A muddy motorbike hovered a few yards behind the cavalcade, refusing to pass even when the riders made room and waved it forward.

The gate was open, and parked beside it was Jonah's Land Rover, with Dora Marshall in the passenger seat and Gus perched on her knee, the empty child-safe carrier wedged between her and the driver.

'Oh, look! There's Mummy,' she trilled, waving out of the window.

Jonah was propped on his crutch as they all hustled through. 'I'll shut it, don't worry,' he called, 'but watch where you go. It's pretty soft on the verges.'

Water lay in great puddles in the fields flanking the marsh where the drainage ditches had flooded in recent rain, and grazing bullocks had poached the gateways fetlock-deep. Lucky Dip, who had been foaled in the Connemara bogs, knew just how to deal with such conditions. She adopted a curious paddling gait which carried her forward without sinking in, but Fireball's extravagant action was far less suited to soft ground. Time and again he stumbled as the turf gave way beneath him.

'Keep to the high ground,' Helen called, and herself edged Lucky Dip towards a line of gorse bushes which seemed to indicate firmer going.

Over her shoulder, she could see several of the Field were in trouble. Isabel's Daisy had plunged into a patch of bog, from which a knot of helpers was trying to extricate her. With reins pulled over her head and hind legs deep in liquid mud, she was refusing steadfastly to move.

'Want a hand?' said courteous Ricky, reining to a halt beside her but Isabel waved him away.

'I can manage, thanks. You go on.'

Other riders soon decided that discretion was the better part of valour and retreated to the road. Helen shaded her eyes and saw that Fergal had lifted his hounds from the swamp and was bringing them round its perimeter to see if they could hit off the line from the other side. The quickest way to rejoin them was to jump two stiff-looking intervening hedges, and she saw from the corner of her eye that this was what Ricky planned to do. It was well within the capability of Lucky Dip, and Democrat was an Intermediate eventer, but what about Fireball? He was a pony, barely 14hh. and the take-off was soft, hardly ideal for a big effort.

'Can you jump that?' she asked. 'If not, we can go round the long way.'

Candy grinned. 'No probs.'

'You're sure?'

'Just give us a lead.'

Helen nodded and approached the hedge at a collected canter. Lucky Dip liked to make her own decisions about when and where to take off, but the extra hoist of her hind legs took her rider by surprise, indicating some unseen obstacle on the landing side. She pecked a little but Helen sat tight and glanced behind in time to see Fireball soaring over the hedge and its invisible overgrown ditch, with a good three inches of air between Candy and the saddle.

'Well sat!' she exclaimed as they landed, still united, and Candy grabbed up the reins she had dropped. 'That was bigger than I expected.'

A glorious thundering gallop across firm old turf rewarded them for taking the shortcut, but as they reached the farther hedge they saw to their disappointment that Fergal and the pack were coming back towards them, having abandoned the swamp.

'Ah, well. As the Good Book tells us, the first shall be last and the last first,' muttered Ricky philosophically as the stalwarts of the road party drew to one side to let them pass, and the whole clattering cavalcade headed for the next draw.

From his high perch on a stack of silage bales, Dragsman One grinned as he watched their withdrawal, and rang his mate.

'Looks like I got them beat good and proper in the marsh. Couldn't hold the line, though I gave them every chance. Not a lot of scent, if you ask me. They're on the lower road now, coming your way. You'd best get weaving.'

'Wilco,' said Dragsman Two, who trained SAS recruits in the Brecon Beacons and had been a champion long-distance runner. He picked up the foul-smelling bag of aniseed-soaked bran mixed with wolf urine begged from a zoo. Charlene's really gonna love me tonight, he thought, as he attached it to the harness on his belt and slid down his own high bale-stack to the ground. He set off at a steady jog across sticky winter stubbles towards a new plantation on the edge of the beech-wood. Plenty of scope for evasion and escape in there, he reckoned.

*****

Snug in the lair of dead bracken he had made for himself between the thick trunks and lower branches of the spruce shelterbelt which protected the Lime Paddock from the prevailing wind, Robb was prepared for a long vigil. He had taken up his position before daylight, parking the car at the station a mile away, and after making an indirect approach through the woods was confident that no one had seen him settle where he could monitor not only Suleiman's paddock but that of the two brood mares and sundry young horses who were also out at grass.

Although there had been a perfectly adequate three-foot six wooden railing fence round the paddock when Suleiman arrived at Barleycourt, Isabel had insisted it was too low. She persuaded Jonah to raise it another two foot and beef up the railings – 'Don't worry, darling, I'll pay,' – and this secure, isolated, four-acre enclosure had since become the stallion's private fiefdom which no other horses were permitted to graze. Sarah, the donkey, kept him company, wearing a muzzle that restricted the amount of grass she could consume, but like all donkeys she had ways and means of dodging measures imposed for her own good, and could often be seen with the muzzle hanging uselessly from the straps that were meant to keep it in place while she stuffed herself with grass.

Robb watched Sarah now, working away at a fence post in what was evidently a well-practised routine, rubbing the headpiece of the muzzle and giving it little jerks to test the breaking strain.

Down at the empty stables, Jim Winter was keeping an eye on the yard from a similar hideout in the hayloft. He had observed unobserved the early hustle and bustle of feeding, grooming, tacking-up and marvelled that so many people could spend so much time and effort, not to mention money, on what – to him – barely qualified as a sport. He preferred a solo challenge: mountain biking or paragliding; diving to explore sunken wrecks, or martial arts contests. The bruises from his encounter with the shaven-headed Chinese gatekeeper had begun to turn from purple to greeny-yellow, but any unwary movement of his right arm still gave his collarbone a sharp twinge and revived his frustration that he had been so easily bested. The fear of joining William Yu in that stinking inspection pit would haunt his dreams for a long time yet.

The laden lorries rumbled away, soon followed by Jonah Murray with his crutch and the little boy strapped into the Land Rover's child safety seat, and peace descended on the yard. He texted Robb: *All quiet here*, and got a one-word response: *Ditto*. Then he settled down to wait.

Armoured against cold by long johns, thermal vest and padded trousers, Robb, too, was thinking of the raid on the Confucius Centre and its aftermath. As he expected, it had caused a diplomatic stink. Presented with evidence of Mr Li's guilt, the Foreign Office had no option but to summon the Chinese ambassador, who had equally little choice in how to respond. Rather than see Mr Li in court, he had announced that the Centre was to close with immediate effect, and all its personnel would leave the country in the next week. William Yu had agreed not to press charges, and the matter of illegal trading in wild animal skins was conveniently swept under the carpet.

A fudge, thought Robb, but what did I expect? A confession? More than ever he was convinced that Anne Cutler had been the target of the bomb in the car park, and Noel the classic 'wrong-place-at-the-wrong-time' collateral damage, but he had no evidence. There would probably never be any. He regretted now that he had never come to know his son-in-law, by all accounts a very nice guy, but his ingrained prejudice against the horse dealer who seduced away his eldest daughter had blinded him to any good points Noel had. I'm just a bigoted old dinosaur, he thought sadly. If I was a horse I'd be put out to grass – if not sent to the knacker.

Well-hidden as he was in the bracken nest, he was sure the horses were aware they were being watched. From time to time Suleiman would raise his head from the grass and survey his surroundings, taking in the whole sweep of fields, woods, grazing animals, and paying particular attention to where Robb was concealed, before resuming his steady munching. Sarah continued to work patiently at breaking the strap of her muzzle.

Robb brooded. He knew his late wife, Meriel, would have spotted instantly whether or not Noel was a wrong 'un. She had always been better than he was at interpreting character, and she'd rarely been wrong about the personalities of their daughters' boyfriends. He remembered her dismissing one as a chancer and another as 'a five-furlong man: wouldn't last the full mile', and subtly discouraging one or other of the girls from pursuing the relationship. It was only after her death that he realised just how much he had come to rely on her judgment and for the thousandth time he cursed his split-second decision to put her in the passenger seat of her car instead of letting her drive home after visiting friends. Now that he had to deal alone with what was for him alien territory, it was hardly surprising that he had made the wrong call regarding Helen's love life.

Like any father, all he wanted was to see his daughters happy, though of course he wanted them to forge successful careers, too. To succeed in whatever field they chose, and never to be financially dependent on a man. Here at Barleycourt Helen worked all hours and never seemed to resent how little she earned; she was well-liked and good at her job. Could he, Robb, ever persuade himself that this life suited her better than making squillions in an office?

The whole question was beyond him. He put it aside and turned his attention to the bomb's other victim. Anne Cutler had worked for the Chinese, although both her sister and her daughter knew she didn't like them or the hectoring, proselytising tone of the lecturers who came and went from the Confucius Centre. She spoke Mandarin and a smattering of Cantonese. Could she have been placed there as a mole to gather information for William Yu's savage editorial attacks on the CCP?

The more Robb considered this hypothesis, the more it appealed to him. If something had blown Anne's cover, Mr Li and his heavies would not have hesitated in eliminating her.

Enquiries by the local police had found no evidence that Norrie MacAleese was anywhere but in the place he claimed to be at the time of the bombing, two hundred miles away in North Yorkshire. No one who knew of his murky past thought it likely that he would pursue a feud with explosives. He had no quarrel with Anne Cutler and would not have known which was her car. In short, as a suspect, Norrie MacAleese was a dead duck.

His thoughts turned to William Yu. Now there was an odd one. Battered and bruised and half asphyxiated as he had been when rescued from the garage, he had still been reluctant to press charges against his abductors, saying he preferred not to be identified. He had too many family members at risk in Hong Kong to allow any hint reaching the CCP that he had been the prime cause of getting the Confucius Centre closed.

'Their eyes – and spies – are everywhere, even in England,' he said. 'Already I am too well known for safety, but...' he hesitated, then added – 'I have a particular reason for visiting this area from time to time.'

Not difficult to guess what that is, thought Robb.

Peace and quiet. A weak sun touched his face, welcome in midwinter even if it conveyed little warmth. He stretched out his cramped legs: his early start combined with the comfort of his bracken lair was making him sleepy.

Of course the countryside was never really quiet. He could identify most of the sounds breaking the silence: a faraway tractor with a flail-cutter, slashing hedges. The occasional *pop-pop* from a pigeon shooter. A barking deer. Numerous birds he didn't know by name or call; noisy rooks and mewing buzzards.

Basing it on his experience with Jabez, he tried to work out how long it would be before the riders returned. The Meet had been scheduled for eleven o'clock and already it was nearly one by his watch. Say they spent forty minutes in the town square; another half hour before hounds hit off the first line. A couple of checks; say fifteen minutes combined – then a three mile point. Another half hour. On to pick up the second line: another forty minutes...

It was as bad as counting sheep over a stile. Before he reached the third line, Robb had dozed off.

*****

Dragsman Two had over-estimated his own speed or under-estimated that of Fergal's hounds, who 'bowled him over in the open' – that is to say, caught up with him – before he reached the sanctuary of his 'earth' on Maidenslove Common, where those who aspired to Second Horses expected to swap mounts. This was where many of the Field would decide that enough was enough: they had had two exciting runs with plenty of jumping, and now they would call it a day, hack back quietly to where they had left their lorries or trailers, and head for home, leaving the die-hards on their fresh horses to enjoy the later stages of the hunt.

Helen and Candy watched as Fergal dismounted and made much of his hounds, distributing biscuits and compliments, and the dragsman excused his failure to get to ground by claiming that a blister had slowed him down.

'A likely tale!' scoffed Harvey. 'You want to lose a few pounds, my lad,' which was a bit rich coming from the tubby little whipper-in.

'Want to swap places?' But the former cross-country champ was too blown to pick a fight, and instead accepted a high-protein drink to help him recover.

'Time we were getting back,' said Helen, turning away from hounds and loosening Lucky Dip's girth a couple of holes.

'Just one more line – oh, *please!*' begged Candy. 'Fireball's not a bit tired, and I know they'll be going on to that farm at Kingsleaze which has lots of schooling fences. Oh, please, Hels, let me stay out a bit longer. It's only just half past two.'

Helen hesitated. Her worry over leaving Barleycourt unguarded had retreated to the back of her mind while hounds were running, and though it now resurfaced, it was with less immediacy. By now Jonah would surely have tired of her small son's company and taken him home for lunch and a nap. Seamus should be back with his load of straw, and although John and Jeremy would still be waiting at the Meet to drive their liveries back to the stables, there would be enough people around to scare off any intruders.

There was nothing to stop her staying out a bit longer.

'*Please!*' repeated Candy.

She capitulated, and tightened Lucky Dip's girth again. 'Oh, OK then. Just one more.'

The dozen or so Second Horses looked very clean and fresh in contrast to those who had taken part in the morning hunt. Like Candy, their riders had hoped hounds would head for the Equestrian Centre at Kingsleaze Farm, where they could have a crack at the newly installed cross-country fences, but after weeks of wet weather the ground was so soft that the owner had refused to let more than a few horses on to the course.

'Any other time, you'd be welcome,' he told the Hunt Committee, 'but we don't want the take-offs poached to glory just weeks before our first One Day Event. Wait until you're down to single figures for the last line, and you can have a jolly going round our fences before blowing for home.'

So there was a palpable sense of disappointment when Fergal led his pack straight past the fingerpost to Kingsleaze, and headed once again for Castle Marsh.

Candy was downcast. 'This is the wrong way,' she complained.

'I know. It's a pity, but my guess is that the ground's so wet at Kingsleaze that all these horses would cut it up badly. At least we can't do any damage round the marsh.'

For the best part of an hour hounds puzzled out the complicated trail the runner had laid around the rushy verges, and the Field moved slowly after them. For anyone interested in hound-work, it was fascinating to watch, but a growing frustration for those who wanted to gallop and jump. In ones and twos they said good night and turned away, so when Fergal finally called his hounds off no more than eight horsemen were still with them.

'Now we can go to Kingsleaze,' said Candy, but Helen shook her head.

'Sorry, but no. I said just one more line, and we've had that. Now we're going home. Fireball's tired. He's carried you long enough.'

'He's not! He never gets tired.'

'Come on, Candy, be your age,' said Helen sharply. 'Five hours is quite long enough for any horse, and besides there's lots to do when we get home.'

'Okey-dokey.' Despite her explosive temper, Candy was no sulker. With a gusty sigh, she turned Fireball away from the other horses, eased his girth, and followed Lucky Dip towards the castle.

'You'll get plenty more chances to try out the Kingsleaze course.' Helen fumbled with icy fingers for her phone. 'I'm going to ring Jem and ask him to pick us up with the trailer. All the others will have gone back in the lorry by now. By the way, what were you about to say about your Uncle William, just before we moved off?'

'Was I? ' said Candy vaguely. 'I don't remember. Nothing that matters, anyway.'

They both dismounted and walked a mile, partly to thaw out their cold feet and partly to ease the horses. Candy varied her trudging with the occasional skip: she had enjoyed the day and wished it could have gone on for ever. Turning to Helen, she said impulsively, 'You won't let Aunt Prue take me back to London, will you? She says I'd like it there, but I really wouldn't. So long as I can stay with you and help with Gus I shall be perfectly happy.'

'That's a deal, then,' said Helen, curiously touched.

She didn't hear Candy add under her breath, 'And from time to time my father will come to meet me.'

\*\*\*\*\*

Summer skies. Tea on the terrace at his grandparents' home, with a home-made cake and a big chunk of honeycomb.

'Don't bring that out here, Mary,' fretted Grandpa Tom. 'We'll have every bee in the garden wanting to share it with us.'

But the bees had already smelled the comb, and were darkening the sky, buzzing round them in a thickening swarm that grew ever louder...

Robb woke with a start. The buzzing sound was not inside his head, but coming from behind the dense leylandii hedge that sheltered the Lime Paddock from the north wind. The donkey had heard it, too, and so had the stallion. He stood rigidly at gaze, head and tail up, staring in the direction of the threat. It grew louder, then faded, then returned.

A drone, thought Robb, with sudden recognition. A drone searching for something. He looked up, scanning the sky, but could see nothing. Suleiman was clearly agitated. He began to pace back and forth, guarding his donkey, and blasted two loud snorts from his nostrils to challenge the unseen intruder. Then Robb saw the drone appear high above the leylandii hedge, small at first, but rapidly descending: a monstrous buzzing insect with four wings and rigid legs. It hovered for an instant, then flew straight towards the horse, circled round his head and was gone.

The stallion went mad. He crouched with all four legs bent as if he meant to roll, then reared, striking out with his hoofs and shaking his head, ears flat back and nostrils flaring. Again the drone zoomed over the hedge and targeted him, following as he squealed and tried to out-run it, thundering across the paddock at a flat-out gallop, eyes wild, mane and tail streaming.

My God, he's going to try to jump, thought Robb, watching helplessly. But even in his panic the stallion must have realised the reinforced rails were too high. He skidded to a halt just before hitting them, wheeled, and raced back to try the other side of the field. The drone followed. The donkey brayed heartrendingly, again and again, cantering in small circles, unable to keep up.

Back and forth Suleiman galloped, making great skid marks in the turf each time he turned, and every moment Robb expected him to lose his footing and crash to the ground. There was nothing he could do to stop his wild career. The horse was beyond reason: sooner or later, he thought, this is going to end in tragedy. He had seen Helen carefully lock the gate, hoping to ensure her charge's safety, but by doing so she had removed any possibility of letting him escape the tormenting drone.

Where was it coming from? Who was directing it? The buzzing sounded far off one minute and very close the next.

'Jim, I need you,' he said urgently into his phone. 'Get up to the Lime Paddock – quick!' Maybe with Winter's help he could lift the gate off its hinges, catch the donkey's headcollar and hope the stallion would follow her into the woods, where the drone could no longer see him.

He lost count of time as the deadly game continued. The donkey brayed again and again and Robb could see the horse was tiring, beginning to stumble. The drone changed its tactics, hovering twenty feet over Suleiman's head like a vast malevolent bee, then turning away to menace the donkey. It had begun to regain height for another run when there was a sudden sharp report. It lurched lopsidedly and began to spin.

Winged, thought Robb, with a leap of hope.

A second shot and it crashed to the ground.

Robb let out a sigh of relief and stared around trying to see where the shot had come from.

'Hey, you!' shouted a camo-clad young man, standing by the locked gate. He broke his gun and climbed over. 'Sit and stay,' he ordered his spaniel, picked up the gun, and stormed across to confront Robb.

'You bloody fool! What the hell d'you think you're doing? You've frightened that horse half to death,' he said angrily. 'You can't fly drones near animals. Who the hell are you?' He stared at Robb, frowning, and a flicker of recognition came into his eyes. 'Oh! I've seen you before. Aren't you –?'

'Helen's father,' said Robb.

'DCI Robb?'

'That's right. And you?'

'I'm Piers Marshall. Jonah lets me shoot his pigeons. But why on earth –?'

Robb found he was shaking. He said unsteadily, 'My daughter asked me to keep a watch on that horse while everybody was out today, because there have been a couple of nasty incidents involving him lately. So that's what I was doing – keeping him safe. Lovely job I made of it! Letting him be attacked by a drone. Thank God you shot it down before he injured himself.'

They both looked over at the horse, who was recovering from his fright. Though his flanks still pumped in and out his eyes were no longer wild. He was grazing so close to his companion that their noses nearly touched. Sarah had succeeded in breaking the headpiece of her muzzle, which hung down uselessly as she tore out great mouthfuls of grass.

Piers searched his pocket and took out a roll. 'Hey, Sarah, want a Polo?'

She lifted her head as he walked over to her, and the stallion approached for his share.

'No damage that I can see,' said Piers after a quick inspection, 'but that was a near thing. I've never heard a donkey make such a rumpus, and Suleiman was going like the clappers.'

'I was afraid he'd run into the fence,' said Robb. 'I couldn't see how to stop him.'

Together they inspected the crashed drone. Piers's shots had shattered the camera and two of the four struts and made a gaping hole in the fuselage. It would never fly again.

'Nice shooting,' said Robb.

Piers ducked his head deprecatingly. 'Nice target.'

'*Optimus 6K* – that's quite a serious piece of kit. Someone really meant business. But who? And where is he?'

Piers shrugged. 'Could be anywhere. My guess is he's seen what's happened and scarpered. Or is hiding.'

'Hmm… Well, my sergeant's on his way to join me, and perhaps the three of us can flush him out.'

'I'll get my dog. Trouble is, those things have a long range – he could be anywhere within a couple of miles. Hey, what's that?' He spun round to face the leylandii hedge as the low growl of a scrambler bike started up behind it. 'Listen, I bet that's him! Quick, let's look!'

But forcing through the tight-packed evergreen branches was almost impossible. The tops had been trimmed dead level at nine foot and grown into a dense windproof barrier.

'Leg me up.' Piers was almost dancing with frustration. 'Quick, take my gun and give me your binocs.'

Swiftly Robb bent and with Piers' foot in his joined hands, flung him up to land on top of the hedge. He scrambled up unsteadily, found a solid spot to balance, and trained the binoculars on the fast-disappearing motorbike.

'He's making for the lane into the wood. I can't see who – but I know that bike… *Oh, God!*'

He turned a stricken face to Robb, who had also heard the crash. 'What was that? What's happened?' he asked urgently.

Piers slid to the ground, white-faced. 'He hit a Land Rover just beyond the gate. It was coming up the lane and hadn't a hope of stopping. The b-bike…' he stammered – 'w-went straight into it…'

They ran across the paddock and climbed the gate. With the spaniel at their heels they hurried along the muddy, potholed lane to where they could see a Land Rover with its driver's door open, a scrambler bike with its wheels still spinning and, kneeling a few yards away, Jim Winter attempting to resuscitate the crumpled figure of Jago Smith.

# CHAPTER ELEVEN

FOUR DAYS LATER, Helen and Jonah leaned on the locked gate of the Lime Paddock, looking at the stallion and his donkey standing head to tail, peacefully nibbling at one another's withers.

'So beautiful,' said Jonah, though his eyes were not on the animals.

'Such a worry,' she responded.

'Suleiman? Well, he's not going to worry you much longer.'

She swung round to look at him directly. 'What do you mean?'

'Izzy rang last night to tell me she has sold him.' Jonah's tone was studiedly neutral. 'She wants to forget about dressage and turn her full attention to owning and breeding racehorses.'

It was the last thing Helen had expected. For a moment she was speechless, unable to decide whether she was pleased or horrified by the news. Relieved, certainly, but also indignant on the stallion's behalf that he should be tossed aside on a whim, converted into cash to pay for another type of horse. Hadn't they taken enough care of him? Wouldn't John and Jeremy feel offended and hurt to watch him summarily removed?

To cover her confusion she asked, 'Who's bought him? And what about Sarah?'

Jonah smiled. 'Sarah, I am glad to say, is included in the deal. You don't break up that kind of love affair lightly. As for the buyer, Izzy was pretty cagey but I think – I'm almost certain – that it is the American girl who won silver at the Baden-Baden championships last summer. Martha Kinnerton. She's got some good horses and her father owns a stud farm in Virginia. Whether she bought him outright or some plutocrat helped her wasn't clear, but she's definitely going to ride him.'

He paused, then added, 'I think dear Izzy has collided with reality at last, and sees that she is never going to reach the very top herself. She hasn't the determination, dedication, and all that. She simply doesn't care enough.'

Helen drew a deep breath and let it out slowly. Jonah watched her with interest. 'Are you pleased?'

'Well...' She paused – a long, long pause – before adding, 'Yes and no.'

He said with mock indignation, 'You are the limit! For nearly four months you've been badgering me to get that horse removed, and now when I tell you he's going, you're having second thoughts.'

'Not really. But...'

He said quickly, 'I know exactly how you feel. We'll get used to it. We'll watch from afar as he conquers the world, which he is much more likely to do without Isabel's involvement.'

She nodded without speaking, and looked back at Suleiman, who was harassing the donkey with little nips, inciting her to play. His burnished chestnut coat shone in the sun and every movement was as graceful as a ballet dancer's. Yes, she would miss him. The stable yard would be a more humdrum, workaday place without such a star to light it up.

What she would not miss was the constant anxiety of keeping him safe and well. He would be better off at stud.

Jonah said briskly, 'So that's the good news.'

'What's the bad?'

'Your father is feeling the irresistible pull of work. He wants to leave after lunch today. I tried to persuade him to stay a bit longer, but he told me to tell you that he had changed his mind.'

'Oh?'

'He said he was quite happy now to leave you and Gus in my care, because he was sure I would look after you. Now what do you think he meant by that?'

Helen flashed him a sideways glance and smiled.

'I haven't the faintest idea,' she said.

---